THE TALE OF HODGEPODGE

A LOST HIPPO, A POETRY-SPOUTING PARROT, AND THE QUEST FOR THE WOW

GEOFFERY ALAN MOORE

Illustrated by Heather Bousquet

The Living Conversation

Copyright © 2020

Text © Geoffery Alan Moore

Illustrations © Heather Bousquet

All rights reserved. Except as permitted under U.S. Copyright Act of 1976, no part of this publication may be reproduced, distributed, or transmitted in any form or by any means, or stored in a database or retrieval system, without the prior written permission of the publisher.

Published in the United States of America 2020
by Living Conversation Books
136 S Patterson Park Avenue, Baltimore, MD 21231
Visit our website at www.TheLivingConversation.com

Visit Geoffery Alan Moore's website at
www.GeofferyMoore.com

ISBN: 978-0-9964978-2-4

Printed in the United States of America

Book and Cover Design by Elise Grinstead of Elisign Design

First Edition: July 2020

10 9 8 7 6 5 4 3 2 1

For Ivy, Iris, Archer, and Mirabel
My four amusing muses

To Connie,
Hope you enjoy the story — ~~for~~ joy is the point of our journey

Geoff Hanttula

*And when you find yourself in the place just right,
You will be in the valley of love and delight.*
—FROM THE HYMN, 'TIS THE GIFT TO BE SIMPLE

*Here and now, here and now,
The place and time to find your Wow;
And when you find your Wow in the now,
You'll be the master of What and How.*
—KRAKATOA THE PARROT-POET

Prologue

● ● ●

EXPLORERS SAY THAT THE SMALL VILLAGE OF BAHATI IN DEEPEST, DARKEST AFRICA JUST HAPPENS TO BE ONE OF THE HAPPIEST PLACES ON EARTH.

But that is not the most remarkable thing.

They also say that if you go to the village square, you will see a life-sized statue of a hippo with a parrot on its head.

But that is also not the most remarkable thing.

Here is the most remarkable thing: Once a year, the people of the village come together to hear the story of that hippo. And this has happened every year in Bahati for over a thousand years.

The story is called The Tale of Hodgepodge. It is still being told today. And it happens like this:

At sunset on the last night of the year, the people gather in the village square around a big bonfire. When all is quiet, Hekima, the oldest man in the village, stands up. His face is dark and wrinkled, but his boyish eyes are bright and dancing. His voice is warm and deep and his broad smile seems to glow in the dark.

"Welcome, my friends," says Hekima. "Before we begin the story, I want to remind you that—according to legend—our ancient ancestor first heard this tale from a parrot with one green eye and one blue eye. And since this happened long ago in the time of the Wow Magic, anything is possible."

And then, Hekima begins.

CHAPTER ONE
"IT MUST BE A SON!"

"The river is beautiful, peaceful, delightful. But it also contains crocodiles. It is a lot like life."
—KRAKATOA THE PARROT-POET

LONG, LONG AGO, when even the animals had dreams and believed in them, a father and mother hippo were standing at the edge of a wide river that bordered a vast jungle. They were watching their daughter Sunshine play in the water with the other hippos. And they were talking about their second child, soon to be born.

Bull, the father—a huge hippo and the leader of the tribe—raised his head to the sky and said in a commanding voice: "It must be a son! It *will* be a son!"

"Well, as long as you're giving orders to the universe, dear—why don't you place an order for the baby to come today?"

said Moon, the mother. "It feels like I have a boulder in my belly. Just look at me: I'm as big as a whale!"

"My dear, you do not look like a whale," said Bull. "You are as lovely as a field of flowers, as sweet as a pineapple."

"Uh-huh, all you think about is food," she said, grinning.

"I protest! My love for you is as eternal as … as eternal as the morning sun."

"Sweetheart, it's nice to know that your love for me is eternal, but right now I just need one hour of your time. I'd love to climb up on the bank and let the sun warm these aching muscles. Do you think you can watch Sunshine and be boss of the universe at the same time?"

"Yes—of course, of course," said Bull. Then he announced to his daughter, "Sunshine, your father will be watching you now!"

Moon looked at Bull. "Are you *sure* you can keep up with her?"

"Don't worry! Don't worry!"

But Moon did worry—for two important reasons.

She worried because Sunshine was a curious, adventurous child who loved to explore up and down the river. Moon's greatest fear was that her daughter would wander off chasing butterflies or other whims and be attacked by crocodiles who prowled the river hoping to catch a young hippo alone.

And she worried about Bull. As the leader, he had always

protected them from the crocodiles. But now he was getting older and slower. And taking long naps during the day. And giving orders to no one in particular.

Once, Bull's great roar would send the crocodiles scurrying away like frightened cockroaches. But now when he roared, the crocs only laughed.

To be safe, Moon reminded Sunshine again, "Stay with the others—do you hear me, darling? Don't even think about going off by yourself!"

"Yes, Mama," said Sunshine.

"And what do you do if you see a crocodile?"

"Get away fast!"

"That's right! Fly away like a bird."

"I will, Mama."

Moon climbed and struggled and pushed her heavy body up onto the high bank. She found a sunny spot where she could lay down and warm her aching bones and, oh, did it feel good!

She got comfortable and looked out at the river. The morning sunlight danced on the water. A snow-white egret coasted down as quietly as a whisper and landed softly at the water's edge. A large fish jumped for joy. But the river paid no attention; it kept on flowing silently and powerfully, keeping its secrets as it had for thousands of years.

Moon sighed. At moments like these, she felt especially

close to the Wow Spirit—the Spirit in all things that makes them marvelous, mysterious, and magical.

She often told Sunshine, "Always listen to the Wow inside you, my child, and always listen to your dreams. It is through our dreams that the Wow Spirit reaches us and guides us."

Then, Moon's thoughts turned to the "boulder" in her belly. Like Bull, she hoped it would be a son who would grow up strong and brave to help fight the crocodiles.

While Moon was thinking about this, two things happened at once.

First, she suddenly realized she was very hungry. And second, at the same moment, there was a sharp pain in her belly.

"Ohhhh!" she moaned. "Are you hungry too, my little boulder? Don't worry—Mama will find us something good to eat. We must keep you growing strong."

Moon struggled to her feet and looked out across the river. Her small ears twitched and her head turned left and right as she watched for any movement, any sign of a crocodile. When she was sure that all was well, she called out: "Bull, I need to find something to eat. Are you sure you're all right?"

"Everything is perfect," Bull called back. "I order you to go!"

"You won't take a nap while I'm gone?"

"No, no, no. Wide awake! On the job!"

Moon started to go, but a small alarm in her mind made her turn back to watch Bull and Sunshine for just a little longer as they splashed playfully in the river. *I wish I could hold onto this moment,* she thought. *Everything I love is here and now.*

Moon looked around. There was nothing to eat on the muddy bank. Down at the river's edge there was delicious grass, of course, but she wasn't ready to leave the warmth of the sun and get back in the river just yet. It had been hard work pushing her heavy body up onto the high bank and she didn't want to do it all over again.

"Ohhh!" Moon moaned after another sharp pain in her belly.

If she was going to find some food quickly, there was only one place to look.

She turned and entered the dense, dark jungle.

And disappeared.

CHAPTER TWO

"MERCIFUL SKIES, WHAT IS THIS HOMELY THING?"

"Everyone has to start somewhere."
—KRAKATOA THE PARROT-POET

"**BUMPSTER BAGLEY! GET YOUR CURLY** little tail back here right now! It's mud bath time."

Moxie, the huge mother elephant, only used both of her son's names when he misbehaved. But Bump, as he was usually called, was not listening—as usual. He was headed into the jungle that bordered the broad, flat, grassy savanna where they lived.

Moxie lumbered into the trees after him, flapping her big ears and swinging her trunk from side to side, muttering, "That child is wilder than a pack of jackals." Then she yelled, "Bumpster Bagley! Do you hear me?"

Bump did hear but he didn't answer. A black bird with red wings had told him, "There is someone in the jungle who needs help. Please hurry!" Following the bird, Bump plunged farther into the jungle with his mama crashing and thrashing behind.

When he reached the place, Bump yelled, "Mama, come look!" Mama Moxie arrived moments later. "Bumpster Bagley, you know you're not supposed to run off into the jungle—" and then she stopped. "Merciful skies, what is this homely thing?"

Sitting at the base of a tree was the oddest-looking creature she had ever seen. It was almost as big as Bump, with a fat, oblong body; short, stubby legs; tiny pink ears; a huge, ugly snout; and small, dark, frightened eyes.

And it had just begun to make a bawling racket!

Then Moxie and Bump both noticed what the creature was wailing about: Two small lizards were hissing at him.

"He's afraid of the lizards, Mama," said Bump.

"Get away you rascals!" Moxie said, swinging her trunk and knocking the lizards off into the jungle, squealing as they went. The odd-looking creature stopped bawling, but he was still sobbing and sniffling.

"A bird told me about it, Mama. That's why I came. What is it, Mama?"

Now it might seem strange today but, in that long-ago time, Moxie had never seen or heard of a hippo. So the sight of this odd-looking creature (who was, indeed, a baby hippo) was puzzling.

Moxie answered, "I don't know what on earth it is, but I know a hungry baby when I see one." She moved closer and the creature eagerly started nursing.

"Mercy me—the poor child is starved," Moxie said. "He must have been wandering around in the jungle for days without anything to eat, just looking for his mother. It's a wonder he wasn't killed by a leopard or swallowed by a boa constrictor."

"What happened to his mother, Mama?"

Moxie looked at the dark jungle around them. "I don't know, child. I just don't know."

"Can we keep him, Mama?" Bump said. "I found him!"

"Well, we can't leave him here to get eaten by hyenas, can we? I suppose we can watch him until his mother shows up."

When the little creature finished nursing, he nuzzled up against Moxie and she caressed him gently with her trunk.

"He likes you, Mama," said Bump.

"Come on, little one. You come with us now." Moxie nudged the little lost stranger with her trunk and slowly they made their way back out of the jungle to the elephants' home on the savanna.

CHAPTER THREE

HOW HODGEPODGE GOT HIS NAME

"Being different is not a bad thing. Being different just means you're you and nobody else."
—KRAKATOA THE PARROT-POET

WHEN MOXIE BROUGHT THE ODD-LOOKING little creature back to the savanna, the other animals had no idea what it was. They had never seen or heard of a hippo either and they knew exactly *nothing* about him.

And yet, to hear them talk, you would think that they were experts on the strange newcomer. During evenings at the watering hole, the gossip flew back and forth faster than a bat chasing mosquitos.

"That thing is going to be trouble," said Scab the camel. "You can tell just by looking at him."

"I think I've seen one of those before," said Grace the heron. "It's a cross between a pig and a platypus."

"Nah, it's some kind of gigantic slug," said Riffraff the zebra. "Definitely in the slug family."

"Well, I think it's kind of cute," said Olivia the ostrich.

"Cute? That thing is uglier than a warthog walking backward," said Norton the wildebeest.

"Hey!" said Clyde the warthog. "I'm right here. I can hear you."

"It's just too different. I don't like things that are too different. They make me nervous," said Fidget the gazelle.

"A fly with hiccups makes *you* nervous," said Muzzle the tortoise.

"Well, I never!" said Fidget.

"Obviously, that thing doesn't belong here," said Norton the wildebeest.

"Norton is right. If we let one of these things in here now, pretty soon we'll be overrun by them and they'll cause all kinds of trouble," said Scab the camel.

"Oh, bish bosh!" said Muzzle, the tortoise. "He's just a kid!"

"What are we going to call it?" said Riffraff the Zebra.

Sitting on the ground at the water's edge, Humdrum the monkey looked around with his large, brown eyes and said: "Well, look at him. He's poorly designed. Very impractical. Stubby legs too small to hold up his fat body. Ears and tail look stuck on. Looks like the leftover parts of different animals all crammed together. He's a mixture, a conglomeration. I say we call him Hodgepodge! There you go—that's the ticket."

"I would name it No-neck," said Sniff the giraffe. "Everyone knows: The longer the neck, the greater the intelligence. This thing hardly has any neck at all."

Muzzle, the giant tortoise who claimed to be more than one hundred and fifty years old, craned his wrinkled, leathery neck upward and spoke in a hoarse, gravelly wheeze. "When you've lived as long as I have, Sniff, you will learn that long necks are vastly overrated. Now I—"

Muzzle was interrupted by Scab the camel. "Yes, we all know how terribly old you are, Muzzle," he said, chewing some weeds. "We're all growing old just hearing about it! But is it not true, Muzzle, that out of the one hundred and fifty years you've been in the world, you've spent about one hundred and twenty-five of them inside that ridiculous shell of yours? So in terms of actual world experience, that would make you about twenty-five years old. You're just a child, Muzzle!" Scab grinned.

Muzzle glared at the camel. "You've gone too long without water, Scab. Your brains have dried up."

Scab glared back. "Speaking of brains, your head looks like a butt. And an ugly butt at that."

"When you chew, it looks like your face is throwing a fit!" said Muzzle.

"When you talk, you sound like you're about to croak!" said Scab.

"Humpback!"

"Slowpoke!"

"You, you, you have no respect for your elders, sir—" Muzzle spluttered and promptly pulled into his shell.

Scab grinned triumphantly, showing his crooked, yellow teeth.

At that point, Moxie—who had been listening nearby in the dark—stepped forward and joined them at the watering hole. It suddenly got very quiet.

"Well, I must confess—I am amazed," said Moxie as she looked around. "'What are you amazed about Moxie?' you might ask. I'm amazed at how many opinions you have on a creature you know nothing about. Let me tell you what I know. I know he's just a child. And I know he needs a mother. So I intend to take care of him."

Scab the camel, who regarded himself as the mayor of the watering hole, replied, "Oh yes—you know a lot, Moxie. The real issue, however, is what we do *not* know! We do not know exactly what this Hodgepodge is. We do not know where he came from or what he will do. And I predict he will bring big trouble to the savanna. I say he does not belong here and we should send him back into the jungle!"

At this, everyone started talking at once. Some voiced their support for Scab's opinion and others disagreed.

Moxie calmly raised her trunk and blew a long, loud blast—and everyone stopped talking.

"Say what you want," Moxie said, "This child is part of our family. He's already forgotten about being found in the jungle; he thinks I'm his mother and Bump is his brother. In fact, he seems to think he's an elephant and I'm not going to tell him any differently right now. He's too young to understand. When he's older, I'll tell him and maybe then he'll want to go look for his own kind. But for now, I'm going to raise him like an elephant and anyone who mistreats him will answer to me."

Scab knew he couldn't overrule Moxie but he wanted to have the last word, so he said: "Just make sure this Hodgepodge doesn't cause any trouble."

Then the animals went away for the night, each to its own place, each thinking its own thoughts about the newcomer.

But the name stuck. From that day on they called him Hodgepodge.

CHAPTER FOUR
A STREAM OF QUESTIONS

"From the seeds of curiosity grow the flowers of wisdom and, sometimes, the weeds of trouble."
—KRAKATOA THE PARROT-POET

IN THE DAYS TO COME, little Hodgepodge followed Moxie everywhere like a small shadow. When other animals approached, he would run underneath Moxie to hide and then peek out shyly to see what was going on. At the watering hole, he stared wide-eyed at the animals who were coming and going and he kept up a constant stream of questions.

"What is that animal with the long, long neck, Mama?" he whispered.

"That's a giraffe, child."

The giraffe spread his front two legs and slowly lowered his head to get a drink. "Does it take a long time for his thoughts to get from his head down to his body? Is that why he moves so slow?"

"I'm not sure, child—"

"Do his thoughts ever get stuck in his neck?"

Moxie had to keep herself from laughing. "The giraffes wouldn't say so. They think they are very intelligent."

"Mama, what is that big, angry-looking animal with the horn on his nose? Did his horn fall off of his head? Is that why he's angry?"

"No, child, that's a rhino, and—"

"What about those stripey animals, Mama? Are they black with white stripes or white with black stripes?"

"Those are zebras child, and I'm not sure—"

"And why don't those big birds ever fly up in the sky? Are they afraid?"

"Child, you will wear me out with all these questions. Now, go on and play."

So the days passed one at a time, as they always do. And one day, Hodgepodge's curiosity overcame his shyness. He asked Moxie if he could go exploring on his own.

Moxie looked at him for a long moment. "I suppose so. But stay out of trouble, do you hear me, child?"

"What trouble, Mama?" Hodgepodge said.

"Just behave yourself—especially around the other animals."

"The animals are trouble, Mama? Which animals?"

"Child, if questions were stars you could fill up the sky. Now go on."

And that is how it started.

CHAPTER FIVE
"YOU, SAD TO SAY, ARE NOT A GIRAFFE!"

Learning what you can't do is only the first step to learning what you can do."
—KRAKATOA THE PARROT-POET

"**STAY OUT OF TROUBLE,** stay out of trouble, stay, stay, staaaaay out of trouble."

Hodgepodge made up this song to sing to himself as he rambled across the savanna. In spite of Moxie's warning, he was in high spirits—and with good reason. He was discovering that there is nothing quite so pleasant as a day of wondering and wandering, of roaming and rambling, of sauntering and searching for things to see and hear and smell and taste.

He was also in high spirits because he had a mission. *I will look out of my own eyes and listen with my own ears and find out which animals are trouble and which animals want to be together-friends and have together-fun,* he thought.

"Stay out of trouble, stay out of trouble, stay, stay, staaaay out of trouble!"

Suddenly, he stopped. Sniff the giraffe was walking by with his slow, stately stride. "They say he is very intelligent," Hodgepodge whispered to himself. "I do not think he is trouble."

But he wanted to be sure, so he scrambled on his short legs to follow the giraffe. Sniff stopped next to a very tall tree. He leaned over, reached out with his long tongue, and began gobbling leaves from a top branch.

Sniff happened to look down and notice Hodgepodge watching him. "Oh, goody, it's the hodgepodge," he said, turning back to the treetops.

"Excuse me—what are you doing?" Hodgepodge said, craning his neck to look up.

"What do you think I'm doing?" Sniff said. "I'm eating." He took another bite.

"Yes, but why are you eating the leaves from the tip-top of the tree?"

Sniff slowly finished chewing. "Well, as anyone with an acorn-full of intelligence knows, the leaves at the top of the tree get the most sunshine—so they are the sweetest and most nourishing. Now, if you don't mind—" He went back to eating. Clearly he did not want to be disturbed.

Hodgepodge's first thought was: *Eating leaves from the top of the tree does not sound like trouble. It sounds delicious.*

His second thought was, *I would love to see what the leaves at the top of the tree taste like.* The more he thought about those leaves, the more his mouth watered. And the more his mouth watered, the more he wanted to try them. But of course, there was no way he could *ever* reach the top of that tall tree.

However, there was a small sapling nearby. *This is more my size*, Hodgepodge thought as he walked over to it. He craned his neck and stretched his head upward, but he could still only reach the leaves near the bottom of the tree. So he put his front feet on the trunk of the small tree and pushed himself upward and upward, walking his front legs up the trunk.

This is especially hard, he thought. He kept pushing with his hind legs, up and up until he was almost standing upright on his back legs with his front legs propped among the branches. Now, he could almost-but-not-quite reach the top leaves.

I shall have to push-stretch myself up further, Hodgepodge thought. So he did, pushing higher and stretching up to reach the top leaves, his body leaning more and more heavily on the trunk of the sapling.

But then—to Hodgepodge's great surprise—the small tree slowly bent over like an actor taking a bow. This lifted Hodgepodge's back legs off the ground so that he was now stuck—his body resting on the trunk of the small bent-over tree.

"Uh-oh," he said. "This is not good."

And before Hodgepodge could even think of something to

do, the small tree began bending lower and lower under little Hodgepodge's weight until his hind legs were up in the air, his front legs stuck in the branches, and his head down toward the ground so that he was almost-but-not-quite upside down.

"Help!" said Hodgepodge.

Sniff looked down, still chewing. "What on earth are you doing?"

"I am trying to taste the leaves from the top of this tree. But, unhappily, the leaves at the top of the tree are now at the bottom of the tree."

At that very moment, the small tree broke in two and Hodgepodge crashed to the ground—head first.

"You ridiculous creature," said Sniff. "Eating leaves from the top of the tree is something only giraffes can do. And you, sad to say, are not a giraffe!"

"Oh. Am I in trouble?"

Sniff did not answer. He simply went off to report Hodgepodge's behavior to Scab the camel.

CHAPTER SIX
THIRTEEN BUGS

"When someone doesn't seem to like you, it might just be indigestion."
—KRAKATOA THE PARROT-POET

ON THE VERY NEXT DAY Hodgepodge was off on another ramble—still curious about which animals were trouble. He saw Humdrum the monkey sitting on a rock, picking bugs out of his fur and he stopped to watch.

The monkey held up an orange, wiggly bug and said, "Eleven"—then popped it into his mouth. It made a crunchy sound when he chewed. Then he pulled out a black bug. "Twelve." He popped that one into his mouth, too, and smacked his lips, revealing bits of bugs stuck in his teeth.

Monkeys are always swinging through the trees and playing games and chasing each other and having very much together-fun, Hodgepodge thought. *I do not think they are trouble.*

But the thing about eating bugs made him wonder.

Humdrum noticed Hodgepodge staring at him. "Yes? Yes? What is it?" he said, then added, "Thirteen," and in went a green bug with more crunching.

"Oh, excuse me," said Hodgepodge, trying to think of how to begin. "I, um ... well, could I ask you some questions?"

"Hmph," Humdrum said. "I haven't got time for childish chitchat or trivial titter-tatter or worthless jibber-jabber. I have things to do, things to count. You run along and ... um ... do something." He went back to scratching himself and poking around in his fur, looking for bug number fourteen.

I suppose if I ate thirteen bugs, I would be cranky, too, thought Hodgepodge as he continued exploring.

Next, he saw Grace the heron standing alone on one leg, perfectly still, at the edge of the watering hole. *She is so lovely-elegant,* he thought. He wanted to ask her how she was able to stand so still for so long on one leg.

"Um, excuse me," Hodgepodge said. "I was just wondering—"

"Shhh!" Grace whispered, angrily. "You'll scare away the fish!" She turned back to the watering hole.

Hodgepodge watched quietly, thinking, *I do not think standing on one leg is trouble. It looks splendiferous.*

Then he thought, *If I could stand on one leg, perhaps we could be together-friends.*

He walked to the edge of the water and lifted his front right leg. *That's a good start,* he thought. Then he carefully lifted his back left leg. He really had to concentrate, and he wobbled a bit, but he did it. *Just one more leg,* he thought.

But when he tried to lift a third leg, he fell into the water with a big splash.

"Of all things!" Grace said, angrily. "Now I'll have no fish for dinner and my children will go hungry! You need to learn to behave yourself." She flew away.

Hodgepodge sat on the bank to think. He had not figured out which animals were trouble, but he was beginning to wonder if all animals were cranky.

Meanwhile, Grace flew to Moxie and told her what had happened. Trying not to laugh, Moxie said, "Hodgepodge tried to stand on one leg?"

"Yes! He scared away the fish. If you are going to raise that whatever-it-is like an elephant, you should teach him to behave like a proper elephant and keep all four legs on the ground!"

Then she stalked away to report the incident to Scab.

"At lease he admires you," Moxie called after her. But the heron wasn't impressed.

Moxie found Hodgepodge sitting at the edge of the pond. "My child, let me tell you something. We elephants do not stand on one leg."

"Am I in trouble?" said Hodgepodge.

"No, no—you're not in trouble."

"I just wanted to see if Grace and I could be together-friends."

"I know."

Moxie watched Hodgepodge trot away. "He's young, he will learn," she said, trying to convince herself. "These are just the small troubles that come with growing up."

But Moxie did not know—and how could she?—that these small troubles would one day lead to The Big Trouble.

And the first hint of The Big Trouble was about to appear—in the form of a small lizard.

CHAPTER SEVEN

THE LIZARD AND THE WASPS

*"Fear is a strange beast, and the question is:
Are you riding the beast?
Or is the beast riding you?"*
—KRAKATOA THE PARROT-POET

MOXIE WAS RIGHT ABOUT one thing: Little Hodgepodge had completely forgotten about being found in the jungle. In fact, he had even forgotten about the two lizards that frightened him there.

And yet, somehow, the fear of lizards was still inside him. Just a glimpse of one tiny lizard would drive him crazy. And, to make matters worse, the lizards found it very amusing to pop up and scare Hodgepodge and then watch him yell and run away.

It was embarrassing, really, and Moxie often talked with Hodgepodge about this fear. "Child, we elephants do not run away from lizards," she would explain. "You just need to be a little braver. You need to remember that you are much bigger than a lizard, and a lizard cannot really hurt you."

But the talks did not seem to help.

One day, Hodgepodge was chatting with some lovely blue and gold butterflies that had landed on an acacia bush. He poked his nose into the branches.

"You are very beautiful. Would you like to ride on my nose?" he said to one of the butterflies. "We could have some together-fun."

"That's very kind of you," said the butterfly. "But I have so much to do today. Perhaps another time. Please excuse me."

Just then, a purple lizard jumped out of the bush and landed on Hodgepodge's snout. "AAAAUUUUGGGHHH!" Hodgepodge yelled. He shook the lizard away and took off running this way and that.

He ran under the low branch of a tree accidentally knocking a nest to the ground. A huge cloud of angry wasps poured out and chased Hodgepodge, stinging him as the lizard watched on, laughing.

Unable to get away from the wasps, Hodgepodge ran to the watering hole and leapt in, splashing all the animals who were there to get a drink.

Having lost their first victim to the water, the wasps turned their attack on the other animals. The whole community erupted into chaos as gazelles and zebras and elephants and wildebeests and others danced and yelled and flung their horns and trunks and tails trying to get away from the stinging wasps until, finally, they all jumped into the water together! *Ker-splash!*

And my, oh my—you never heard such complaining! You would have thought the world was coming to an end.

"This is an outrage!" said Norton the wildebeest.

"It's that crazy Hodgepodge again," said Riffraff the zebra.

"It's really too much!" said Fidget the gazelle. "After a stressful day running away from cheetahs, I need my quiet time at the watering hole. But what do I get instead? Wasps! And chaos! Someone should teach that Hodgepodge how to behave."

Over the next few days, the animals pressured Moxie to tell Hodgepodge he was not an elephant and to send him back into the jungle. But she still refused.

"He's a sensitive child," she said. "If a little lizard upsets him that much, just think how upset he'll be if I tell him he's not an elephant and I'm not his first mother. When he's older, he'll be able to handle it better. I'll tell him then."

But soon, something happened that changed Moxie's mind.

CHAPTER EIGHT
THE WATER FIGHT

"Here is a thing you must know about the world: Sometimes, it will try to make you feel bad about yourself."
—KRAKATOA THE PARROT-POET

A FEW DAYS LATER, BUMP CAME rushing up to his mother as she rested in the shade with Hodgepodge.

"Mama, Mama! There's a big water fight at the watering hole. Can I go? Please?"

"Yes, if you take Hodgepodge with you," said Moxie. "You know how he loves to roll around in the water."

"But Mama—do I have to?" (Bump didn't mind playing with Hodgepodge when it was just the two of them. But when he was with his friends, it was a pain to constantly have to answer questions like: "Why is his nose so small?" and "Why does he talk funny?" and "Why is he so afraid of lizards?")

"I would very much like to go to the water fight, Bumpster," said Hodgepodge. "It sounds like very much together-fun."

Bump started to object some more, but Moxie stopped him. "If you want to go, you have to take Hodgepodge. That's that."

Grudgingly, Bump agreed. The two of them headed toward the watering hole with Moxie following at a distance to keep an eye on things.

Hodgepodge had to trot quickly to keep up with Bump. "Thank you very much for taking me to the water fight, Bumpster," he said.

"I've told you before, don't call me Bumpster. Just Bump!"

"Yes, sorry. I keep forgetting. That's actually a better name. I like it. But what is a water fight, Just Bump?"

"Not Just Bump! Just ... Bump!"

"Yes, that is what I said. Just Bump. A good name."

"No! Not Just Bump. Just ... oh, never mind. Let's just hurry."

They got to the watering hole and all the young elephants were there. Hodgepodge watched in delight and amazement as the elephants filled their trunks with water and sprayed each other. Bump joined in and the air filled with their whoops and trumpets and laughter. A small rainbow appeared in the mist.

"So this is a water fight," Hodgepodge said to himself. "What a happy-excellent thing!"

Eager to join in, Hodgepodge ran down to the edge of the watering hole and filled his mouth with water, then reared back and tried with all his might to blow the water out of his nose the way the elephants did.

But nothing came out.

His face turned red and he started choking and gasping and spluttering and coughing as he rolled over and over in the mud, trying to catch his breath. Finally, lying on his back at the edge of the watering hole, breathing hard, Hodgepodge looked up. All of the young elephants were staring at him. And then they exploded in laughter.

"He looked like a tick about to pop!" said one elephant.

"More like he swallowed a bunch of fire ants!" said another.

"Your brother's funny, Bump," said a third elephant.

"He's not my brother!" blurted out Bump.

"Now that's just about enough of that!" said Moxie, as she lumbered down to the watering hole. "You kids have had enough water fighting for one day. Go back to your mothers now."

After the others left, Hodgepodge turned to Bump. "I'm very sorry I spoiled the water fight, Just Bump."

"It's just ... Bump!" said Bump.

"That is what I said."

"It's just ... never mind," said Bump. "It doesn't matter."

"But why did you say that I am not your brother?"

Moxie took a deep sigh. "Come over here, Hodgepodge. I have something to tell you."

CHAPTER NINE
"IS SOMETHING BAD-WRONG WITH ME?"

"It's not easy to know who you really are, but it's harder to not know who you are."
—KRAKATOA THE PARROT-POET

I'**VE DONE IT AGAIN,** *just like the time with the lizard and the wasps,* Hodgepodge thought. He stood with his head drooping, afraid of what Mama Moxie might say.

"Am I in trouble again?" he said. "Do you want to talk to me about how I spoiled the water fight? Because I'm sorry I spoiled the water fight."

"You didn't spoil the water fight," said Moxie. "You just made it more interesting."

"I did?"

"Yes, you did. Now listen, child, I have something to tell you. Look at yourself in the water."

Hodgepodge looked down at his reflection. *It is just my same face,* he thought. *Why does she want me to look at my same face?*

"Now look at me."

Hodgepodge looked up.

"Now look at yourself again."

Hodgepodge looked down. A fish jumped and the ripples erased his reflection.

"Do you see the difference between you and me?"

Hodgepodge was sure he knew the answer. "I'm little. And you're big."

Moxie sighed. "Look again, child. Look carefully. Do you have a long trunk?"

Hodgepodge wrinkled his nose and said, "No, Mama."

"Do you have big floppy ears?"

He turned his head from side to side, looking at himself. "No, Mama. My ears are little."

"And what does that tell you?"

Hodgepodge fidgeted for a few moments, unsure of what to say. "Um … my ears and trunk will grow large when I get older?"

"No child, they won't."

Hodgepodge's eyes widened. "They won't? I don't understand, Mama. Is something bad-wrong with me?"

"There is nothing wrong with you, my child."

Hodgepodge was very confused. "But Mama—if I can't grow a trunk and big floppy ears, there must be something bad-wrong with me." He looked down at his reflection again and turned his head back and forth, trying to figure out what was wrong.

Moxie replied cautiously: "Listen, my child, what I'm about to tell you is not going to be easy to hear, but you're growing up now and you need to know. It's just that ... well, the thing is ... Hodgepodge, you're not an elephant."

Hodgepodge felt a chill go through his body. "I'm not an elephant?" he whispered. He looked back down at his reflection just to be sure.

"No, darling, you're not."

"But ... but ... what am I?"

Moxie sighed. "Child, to be honest, we are not sure what you are."

"You don't know what I am?"

"Well, your name is Hodgepodge. So let's just say you're a hodgepodge."

"But Mama—I don't want to be a hodgepodge. I want to be an elephant. I want to have big floppy ears and a long trunk just like you."

"I understand," said Moxie. "But the fact is that you are not an elephant. That's why you can't do elephant things—like blow water out of your nose."

Hodgepodge looked across the watering hole and squeezed his eyes shut. *Maybe this is just a bad-sad dream,* he thought. But when he opened his eyes, Mama Moxie was still there and he was still the same with his small ears and small nose.

"How about this? How about you teach me how to be an elephant?"

"Hodgepodge, this is not a thing that can be taught," Moxie said, gently.

"How about I try hard to be an elephant? How about I try especially hard?"

"It is not about how hard you try, my child. It's about what you are." Moxie watched nervously to see how he would take all of this information.

Hodgepodge watched an egret take one, two, three steps. It stabbed at the water and brought up a small, wriggling fish. It swallowed the fish whole.

"This is why no one is ever together-friends with me, isn't it?" Hodgepodge said suddenly, fighting back tears. "It is because I am not really an elephant and no one knows what I am."

"Hodgepodge, child, I'm sure you're going to have lots of friends. And one of these days, you'll find out what you are."

"But how, Mama? How will I ever find out what I am?"

"Remember when I told you about the Wow Spirit and the way it talks to us in our dreams? Maybe someday the Wow Spirit will send you a dream and tell you what you are."

"But I've never had a dream, Mama. What if I don't get a dream?"

"Well, maybe someday you'll find animals like you—and they will tell you what you are."

"But Mama—how do I find my own kind of animals if I don't know what my kind is? Or where they are?"

Moxie didn't have an answer for that. She sighed and looked at Hodgepodge. She didn't want to tell him the rest—but there was no getting around it. "Child, there is something else I must tell you. It is also hard to hear, but you need to hear it."

The curiosity in Hodgepodge's head made him want to know what else Moxie had to say. But the empty feeling in his stomach made him afraid to hear it.

Moxie paused and then said, "Hodgepodge, I love you—but you need to understand what this means. It means I'm not your first mother."

Hodgepodge's eyes got even wider. "What do you mean, Mama? I don't understand."

"Well, I'm your second mother. You had another mother before me—your first mother." As gently as she could, Moxie told Hodgepodge the story of how she found him alone in the jungle and raised him as her own.

"I always thought your first mother would come back for you," Moxie explained. "But she never did. At least, not yet."

This was just too much, and now the tears came. "Why did my first mama leave me in the jungle?" Hodgepodge sobbed. "Why didn't she come find me? Didn't she like me? Is it because I always get scared of lizards? Is it because I always get into trouble and no one wants to be together-friends with me?"

Moxie nuzzled him with her trunk. "Oh, my child, I'm sure she loves you just the way you are. Just like I do."

Hodgepodge stopped crying and said, "I'll go into the jungle and find my first mama and she will tell me what I am!"

Moxie shook her head. "I can't let you do that, child. Here on the savanna we have a rule against going into the jungle. You could get lost or bitten by a poisonous snake or attacked by a leopard. And remember—the jungle is full of lizards."

"Lizards? There are lizards in the jungle?"

"And a lot of other creatures even more dangerous than lizards."

"But Mama—if I can't go into the jungle, how will I ever find my first mama?"

"You'll just have to wait and hope she comes back."

"But what if she never comes back? What if she doesn't want a child who is afraid of lizards. What if—" At this, Hodgepodge became so upset, he just ran away.

Moxie watched him go. And now there were tears in *her* eyes.

CHAPTER TEN

THE ONLY HODGEPODGE IN THE WORLD

"When you don't know where to go, going somewhere is often better than going nowhere."

—KRAKATOA THE PARROT-POET

IT WAS A HARD THING for Hodgepodge to find out that he was not an elephant. It was harder still to find out that no one knew what he was. But hardest of all was to find out that his first mother left him in the jungle and never came back for him.

It was a lot to think about.

Hodgepodge went to Overlook Hill nearby and climbed to the top because it was a good place to think. Looking down, he could see the beginning of the jungle far below, vast and dark and mysterious—a place of secrets and dangers.

He shivered at the sight and his tiny pink ears twitched.

The sky was big and a gentle breeze was pushing the clouds along. It was quiet.

Suddenly, Hodgepodge yelled as loud as he could: "Mama! Mama! Mama! Are you in there? Are you in the jungle? Can you hear me?"

Maybe the wind will carry my voice, he was thinking. *Or maybe a bird will take my words to my first mama.* (In the time of the Wow magic, birds were known for doing such things.)

"Mama! I am Hodgepodge—I am your child! I'm staying with Mama Moxie, my second mama. She is an elephant. But I'm not an elephant. I don't know what I am, Mama. Can you come to the savanna and tell me what I am?"

Silence.

"Mama, I am not allowed to go into the jungle and find you—but if you come back, I will try hard not to be scared of lizards. I will try very, very hard."

Silence again.

Hodgepodge climbed back down Overlook Hill. When he got to the bottom, he didn't feel like going back home; he decided to go for a walk instead. He walked across the broad, flat, grassy savanna that stretched away to the horizon in every direction—farther than the eye could see.

After a while, he saw a herd of long-legged, big-eyed ostriches running their silly upright run. They were running scared, as if their lives depended on it—but no one was chasing them.

"Silly birds," Hodgepodge muttered.

Farther on, he heard a loud hum and saw that the hum was coming from a large tree up ahead.

"A humming tree?"

As he drew near, Hodgepodge saw the reason for the hum: Hundreds of bees were at work among the tree blossoms, buzzing busily and noisily.

Hodgepodge passed the humming tree and kept walking farther and farther than he had ever walked before. After a long time, he stopped and looked around.

"The world is scary-big," he said to himself. He felt like the only hodgepodge in the world.

He looked down and saw a slug crawling in the grass. "I bet this slug knows his first mama. I bet he has lots of slug friends and does lots of slug things and has lots of slug together-fun."

It's true. Hodgepodge felt lower than a slug.

Then he noticed a feather floating and dancing on the breeze. "What are you so happy about?" he said. "You're just a feather."

Suddenly, the breeze picked up and the feather began to drift away. It was as if the feather was saying, "Come on, Hodgepodge—follow me if you dare." Having nothing better to do, Hodgepodge followed the feather across the savanna.

And then, he saw something shimmering in the distance. Was it a farm? A village? A mirage? He couldn't tell.

Hodgepodge walked toward the vision. As he came closer, he saw that it was an oasis—a large, beautiful garden surrounded by shade trees filled with flowering plants of all kinds. At the center of the garden, there was a bubbling spring that filled a pool and watered the plants.

Hodgepodge was very hot and thirsty after the long walk, so he ran to the pool and had a nice long drink. Then he enjoyed a meal of sweet grass.

When he had eaten his fill, he felt better. He also felt very, very sleepy. So Hodgepodge laid down, cooled by the shade of the trees and soothed by the sound of the bubbling spring, and he fell into a deep, deep sleep.

And he began to dream his very first dream.

CHAPTER ELEVEN
AN ESPECIALLY PECULIAR DREAM

*"It's one thing to have a dream.
It's another thing to understand it.
And hardest of all is to follow it."*
—KRAKATOA THE PARROT-POET

IN THE DREAM, IT WAS *night and Hodgepodge was running alone through a dark jungle. Suddenly, he heard a voice from above saying, "My child!" He looked up but he only saw the full moon.*

Then, to his surprise, a face appeared in the moon. Even more surprising, it looked much like his face.

"A hodgepodge in the moon?" he wondered.

The face spoke. "My child! My child! I am your mother. I am a hippo. And you are a hippo."

"A hippo? What is a hippo, Mama?" said Hodgepodge. But his mother said nothing.

Then Hodgepodge said, "Mama, how can I get to you?"

Her answer was puzzling: "Jump into dream ... save sunshine ... find the place just right."

Monkeys were chattering all around, making a lot of noise, and Hodgepodge wasn't sure he heard correctly. "Mama, I don't understand. What did you say?"

"Jump into dream ... save sunshine ... find the place just right."

Hodgepodge was confused. He asked again: "But how can I get to you?"

This time Hodgepodge heard: *"Jump into dream, save sunshine, find the place just right ... be brave ... don't let fear hold you down ... fly like a bird ... fly, fly, fly."*

Hodgepodge woke up. He yawned and stretched. He went to the spring and splashed cold water on his face—and then it came back to him.

"I had a dream!" he said. "It was my first mama!"

Hodgepodge splashed more cold water on his face. "My mama said that she is a hippo and I'm a hippo." Talking to himself about the dream made it seem more real.

He looked at his reflection in the water and repeated: "I am a hippo. I am a hippo. I am a hippo." It was a strange-sounding word, but it felt good to say it. "I am a hippo!" he yelled.

But there was more: "She told me to jump into the dream—but I was already in the dream. Then she told me to save the sunshine." Hodgepodge looked up toward the sun. It didn't look like it needed saving. "And she told me to find the place just right, but she didn't tell me where it is."

Hodgepodge shook his head. This was an especially peculiar dream.

There was something else in the dream, but what was it? He sat for a while and, finally, he remembered. "When I asked, 'How can I get to you?' she said, 'Fly like a bird. Fly, fly, fly!'"

At that moment, a big, fat bumblebee flew by, wobbling toward some flowers and bumping into petals as it went. Staring at the bumblebee, Hodgepodge suddenly remembered a conversation he had with Moxie when he was younger.

And then the most lumpy, lopsided idea any hippo ever had entered his brain. It was an idea that sounded amazing and miraculous—but it also sounded ridiculous and impossible.

And it would lead Hodgepodge into all kinds of trouble— including The Big Trouble.

CHAPTER TWELVE
HODGEPODGE'S BIG DEBATE WITH HIMSELF

"Sometimes, looking at a bright, shining dream is like looking at the sun. It is blinding."

—KRAKATOA THE PARROT-POET

HERE IS THE CONVERSATION HODGEPODGE remembered when he saw the bumblebee:

"Always listen to your dreams, child," Moxie had told him. "The Wow Spirit talks to us in our dreams to guide and help us."

"How, Mama?"

"Well, for example, when birds fly across the world, the Wow Spirit sends them messages in their dreams to help them find their way back home."

Just then a big bumblebee flew by on its wobbly, zigzag course.

"Hodgepodge, do you see how that bumblebee flies all wobbly?"

"He looks like a stumblebee, Mama."

"Bumblebees are actually too heavy to fly, but when they listen to their dreams, their hearts fill up with the Wow Magic and they can fly. I think this one is still learning—that's why he wobbles."

"Wow," said Hodgepodge.

"So listen to your dreams and follow them and everything will work out fine."

As Hodgepodge left the oasis and began the long walk home, he was thinking about this conversation.

And he was having a big debate with himself.

First he thought: *My mama said, "Fly, fly, fly." Does she want me to fly over the jungle and find her?*

Then he thought: *But it is crazy. I am heavy and I have no wings. And I have never seen hippos flying.*

Then he thought: *My first mama must be able to fly because she was up in the moon.*

Then he thought: *Still, it is mad-crazy.*

Then he thought: *But maybe the Wow Spirit will give me the Wow Magic to help me fly—just like the bumblebees. Then, I could fly over the jungle without breaking the rule and I wouldn't have to see any lizards or get swallowed by a boa constrictor. And when I found my first mama and she saw me flying, she would be amazed and want to stay with me.*

Then he thought: *Even so ...*

Then he thought: *If the Wow Spirit gives me the Wow Magic to help me learn to fly, then all the animals will see me flying and they will not laugh at me.*

On and on Hodgepodge debated with himself like this, all the way across the savanna. The more he thought about the idea of flying, the more he liked it. The more he liked it, the more he *wanted* to believe it. And the more he wanted to believe it—the more he did believe it.

Learning to fly seemed to be the answer to all his problems.

Hodgepodge walked all the way back to Overlook Hill in a good mood. He climbed to the top, still in a good mood. But when he walked to the edge of the cliff and looked down—it was a long way down and there were big rocks at the bottom of the hill.

"That is scary-far," Hodgepodge said. "I shall have to think about this. I shall have to think very hard." He closed his eyes to concentrate and stood there for a long time.

All at once, he leapt ... and fell down, down, down. He could see the rocks rushing up to meet him until, suddenly, an invisible force like a mighty wind lifted him up and he went soaring above Overlook Hill. He flew all the way back to the watering hole. All the animals were there and, as he circled above them, they cheered and chanted, "Hodgepodge! Hodgepodge! Hodgepodge!" Then he flew far, far away out over the jungle, looping and gliding, as light as a feather. And, finally, he saw her. It was his first mama, standing in a wide clearing. She was looking up and calling to him and excited to see him. There were other hippos with her and they were cheering for him, too. He went diving down to meet them ...

"Oh!" Hodgepodge opened his eyes. He was still on the edge of the cliff. Was it a daydream? Did he fall asleep? Was it another dream from the Wow Spirit?

Hodgepodge shook his head, took a deep breath, and said, "If the Wow Spirit wants me to learn to fly and find my first mama, then I must do it!"

He peeked nervously over the edge of the cliff at the rocks far below. "But I do not think I am ready for this flight yet."

CHAPTER THIRTEEN
"SPLAT THE FLYING HIPPO"

"Laughter can heal. It can also wound."
—KRAKATOA THE PARROT-POET

THE NEXT MORNING, HODGEPODGE HURRIED to the watering hole where the animals had gathered for their morning drink and gossip. He went to a large, flat rock at the far bank and scrambled and pushed himself up on top of it. He stood and faced the animals.

"I am not an elephant!" he announced.

"What a shocker!" Scab the camel said under his breath.

"And I'm not a hodgepodge either," Hodgepodge said. "I am a hippo!"

"Hippo? Hippo? What's a hippo?" said Humdrum the monkey.

"Ah yes, hippos," wheezed Muzzle the tortoise. "I believe they're extinct!"

"Hippo sounds quite unintelligent if you ask me," said Sniff the giraffe—though no one had asked him.

Hodgepodge continued. "I have learned what hippos do and I will now give a demonstration." He looked up into the sky and whispered, *"Please help me, Wow Spirit. Please give me the Wow Magic."* Then he ran and leapt off the edge of the rock ... and fell SPLAT onto the muddy bank below.

"We should name him Splat, the Flying Hippo," said Scab. Everyone laughed.

Lying there in the mud, Hodgepodge said to himself, "I guess I need more practice." He hurried away.

CHAPTER FOURTEEN
THINKING ABOUT HONEY

"Don't expect others to understand your dream. After all, you don't always understand it yourself."
—KRAKATOA THE PARROT-POET

AFTER HE CRASHED IN SUCH a spectacular and humiliating way, you might think Hodgepodge would have given up the idea of flying. But he did not.

In fact, crashing at the watering hole only made him all the more determined. For in addition to being a polite hippo, he was also a persistent hippo.

So Hodgepodge practiced flying every day. He tried flying off of big rocks and big logs. He tried flying off of very large tree stumps. He tried flying over bushes and anthills.

And, in every case, the result was always the same: SPLAT!

But he kept trying. And he also began looking for any clue, any secret, *anything* that might help him learn to fly.

One day, he even asked a bumblebee for advice.

"Excuse me," he said to a bee that had landed on an African lily. "How do you fly like that?"

"I don't know. I just do," said the bumblebee.

"But what do you think about when you're flying?" Hodgepodge asked.

"Honey."

"When you're flying, you think about honey?"

"Yup."

"What do you think about when you're not flying?"

"Honey."

"What about when you're sleeping—what do you dream about?"

"Honey."

"So ... you're always thinking about honey?"

"Yup."

Hodgepodge tried thinking about honey, but that didn't help. In fact, nothing helped. He kept trying to fly and he kept crashing.

Meanwhile, with some of the animals becoming more than a little alarmed at Hodgepodge's behavior, Scab the camel called a meeting at the watering hole. The animals gathered in the evening and everyone started talking at once.

"Just the thought of that heavy, oblong, odd-looking creature running around jumping off of things makes me nervous," said Fidget the gazelle.

"A butterfly sneezing makes you nervous," said Muzzle the tortoise. "Everything makes you nervous."

"Well, I never!" said Fidget.

"And I hope you never do!" said Muzzle.

"But Fidget is right," said Grace the heron. "Hodgepodge scared away all my fish. And I've heard he tried to fly over Olivia the ostrich's nest and smashed her egg. She's had her head in the sand ever since."

"That's horrible!" said Fidget. "It makes me even more nervous."

"I told you we should have sent him back into the jungle," said Scab the camel.

"Oh bish, bosh," said Muzzle the tortoise. "He's just a youngster. He lacks experience and wisdom, that's all. Now I could teach him—"

"How to be a butt-face!" Scab the camel interrupted.

"I wouldn't talk, maggot brain," said Muzzle.

"Bloated snail!" said Scab.

"Double hump-back!" said Muzzle.

"Muzzle is half right," said VanDerMugg the rhino. "Hodgepodge needs a teacher, but he needs someone who can teach him how to be a success. I would happily share my thirty-one secrets of success. Number one is—"

Everyone started talking at once to avoid another one of

VanDerMugg's lectures. But then Moxie appeared, and everyone stopped talking.

"My stars, it suddenly got very quiet around here," said Moxie.

"Moxie, we need to talk to you about the hodgepodge," said Humdrum the monkey.

"He is a hippo," said Moxie. "What do you want to talk about?" She was in a cantankerous mood because everyone had been complaining to her about her adopted child.

"Right you are. Right you are," said Humdrum. "It's just that, well, the thing is—no disrespect to you of course; we all know what a good mother you are—but, well, the thing is—"

"Hodgepodge is upsetting everyone!" said Scab.

Again, everyone started talking at once.

Some of these folks are just looking for an excuse to run Hodgepodge off, Moxie thought as she listened to them going on and on.

Finally, after they calmed down, she spoke: "Look, I know you're all upset. But Hodgepodge is not a bad child. He's not. He has a good heart and he's just a little confused right now. I will talk to him. I'll get him to behave himself. I promise."

Moxie walked away, hoping she could deliver on her promise—and more than a little worried about what might happen if she couldn't.

CHAPTER FIFTEEN

"NOT MY MOST FAVORITE DAY."

*"The brain is a tricky thing.
So don't believe everything you think."*
—KRAKATOA THE PARROT-POET

THE NEXT MORNING, HODGEPODGE WOKE up early, bruised and aching from his latest crash landings. He limped back to Overlook Hill, then climbed to the top. He sat at the edge of the cliff and looked down at the jungle.

"Mama, I'm sorry," Hodgepodge called out. "I am trying to learn to fly and come find you, but I have not yet learned how to do it. It is a scary-hard thing to learn."

Silence.

"Mama, I will try harder, I promise. I will be brave and try especially hard. I will make you proud. I will find you!"

Again, only silence.

"Mama, could you ask the Wow Spirit to give me the Wow

Magic to help me fly? Maybe she is asleep. Or maybe she forgot."

More silence.

Hodgepodge sat there for a long time, looking at the jungle and listening to the wind blow through the trees. Some dark clouds drifted across the sky and hid the sun. Finally, he climbed down and went home, limping all the way.

As Hodgepodge passed the watering hole, some of the young elephants saw him.

"It's Splat, the flying hippo!" said one of the elephants. "Hey, Splat, fly off a rock."

"Seen any lizards lately, Splat?" said another.

"Hey, Splat," said another. "Blow some water out of your nose."

"My name is Hodgepodge," Hodgepodge said.

The young elephants chanted, "Fat Splat! Fat Splat! Fat Splat!"

Hodgepodge tried to think of something to say—but his mind was blank. So he just kept limping along toward home.

This is not my most favorite day, he thought.

Mama Moxie saw him from a distance, limping slowly, and she went out to meet him. "Where have you been, Hodgepodge?" she asked.

"Nowhere," he mumbled. Understandably, he was in a surly mood.

"Let's go sit in the shade, child. We need to talk." And so they did.

"I'm going to come right to the point," Moxie began. "You must stop all this flying nonsense. It's making some folks think you are crazy."

"I don't care what they think," muttered Hodgepodge. "They call me the Hysterical Hippo. And ... and Fat Splat."

"Well, that's not right. I will certainly speak to them about that," said Moxie. "But you still need to give up on the flying idea."

"But Mama—you told me to listen my dreams. In my dream, I asked my first mama how I could find her and she said to fly like a bird."

Moxie sighed. "But we must face facts, Hodgepodge. You're growing up now and getting heavier every day. You're as heavy as a pile of boulders and nothing that heavy can fly."

"What about the bumblebees?" Hodgepodge said.

"Bumblebees?"

"You told me the bumblebees are too heavy to fly but they learn to fly anyway. Remember what you said?"

"Yes, I do, child, but—"

"You said bumblebees can fly because they listen to their dreams and the Wow Spirit gives them the Wow Magic. I listened to my dream—just like you told me. And someday, the Wow Spirit will help me fly. I just have to keep trying."

Moxie realized that there was absolutely nothing she could say. *Maybe he'll listen to some of the others,* she thought.

As for Hodgepodge, he walked away more determined than ever to learn to fly, and here's why: By trying to convince Moxie, he convinced himself all over again.

And there was also this: the more the other animals teased and ridiculed him, the more determined Hodgepodge was to prove that they were wrong—and he was right.

CHAPTER SIXTEEN

"COUNT!"

"It's good to learn how to count, but it's even better to learn what really counts."
—KRAKATOA THE PARROT-POET

MOXIE ASKED HUMDRUM TO TALK to Hodgepodge. The monkey thought he didn't have time for such foolishness, but when the big elephant glared at him, he scuttled off, muttering, "Hurry, hurry ... busy, busy ... no time to lose."

He looked around near some baobab trees, yelling, "Hodgepodge! Hodgepodge!" A loud THUD shook the ground and Humdrum hurried toward the sound. He found Hodgepodge lying flat on his belly at the base of a very large tree stump. As the monkey watched, the hippo got up and started to climb back up onto the stump. He had shoved some logs and rocks up against the stump to use for steps.

"Wait, wait!" yelled Humdrum. "Come down, come down."

Hodgepodge looked down. "Excuse me, but I very much need my flying practice." With that, Hodgepodge closed his eyes and murmured to himself, "Light as a feather. Light as a feather."

Humdrum interrupted. "No, no, no, no. No time for that," he said, backing away from the stump just to be safe. "No flying. Just talking."

Hodgepodge opened his eyes. "Talking? About what?"

Humdrum waved frantically. "Very important. Hurry down now. But don't fly. Careful, careful. But quickly, quickly. But careful."

Hodgepodge was not really in the mood to talk but, since Humdrum was the head monkey, he made an effort to be respectful. "I suppose I could use a break," he sighed, as he climbed down backward.

"That's the ticket!" said Humdrum. He scratched the top of his head with one hand and his belly with the other and said, "The top and bottom of it, the long and short of it, the over and under of it, the inside and outside of it is this: You must stop flying practice. That's it. There you go. Well, I must be going. Things to do. No time to lose." He turned to leave.

"Stop flying practice?" said Hodgepodge.

"Yes, yes, you got it—there you go. Stop flying practice. That's the ticket." He turned to leave again.

"Have you been talking to Mama Moxie?"

Humdrum turned back. "What's that?"

"Humdrum, I don't mean to be rude, but I can't stop trying to fly. I just can't."

"Hmph! Of course you can, of course you can," said Humdrum. "Easy, easy. Just stay on the ground, you see. Not difficult at all." To illustrate, Humdrum stomped the ground with his feet.

"I *know* how to stay on the ground. I've done it all my life. But I had a dream, and—"

Humdrum snorted. "A dream, you say? No, no, no, that won't do. Nasty things, dreams. Get you thinking. Get you imagining things. Overheat your brain, you see. Forget about dreams, there you go."

"But Mr. Humdrum, if you would just let me explain—"

"No, no. Here's what you do. Don't think. Don't dream. Don't fly. Just count. That's the ticket."

"Count? I don't understand ... count what?"

"Beans. Pebbles. Clouds. Bugs. Spots on a leopard. Stripes on a zebra. Yesterday I counted all the leaves on a tree. Yep, yep. Took all day," he said, proudly.

"You did? You counted all the leaves on a tree?"

"Yep."

"That's amazing ... I guess."

"Thank you, thank you," Humdrum said, quite pleased with himself.

"How many are there?"

"What's that?"

"How many leaves on the tree?"

Humdrum was perplexed. "How many? What a question. I uh ... well, I don't exactly remember."

"You don't remember the number?"

"No, not the *exact* number."

"Oh my," said Hodgepodge. "Just think, after all that hard work and you can't remember the number."

"Well, yes, but the thing is—"

"Perhaps you should stop counting."

"What's that?"

"You want me to stop trying to fly. Maybe you should stop counting."

"Stop counting? Rotten maggots, what a thought. No, no, no. Can't do that. I'll just count them again. There you go. That's the beauty of it. Never done counting."

"Okay. So perhaps we could make an agreement: You keep counting and I'll keep learning to fly."

Now Humdrum was really flustered. "No, no, no, no, no. You've got it all wrong, Hodgepodge. You're not paying attention. Here is what I'm saying: I'll stop flying and you ... no, no, that's not it. You stop flying and I'll keep counting."

"But, Humdrum—if you don't remember the number, why do you count at all?"

Humdrum looked confused. This was a question he had never thought about. "Well, uh ... that is ... I count things because .... well, because they are there! There you go. That's it." He was thrilled that he had come up with the answer.

"I see. You count them because they are there."

"Yes, yes, that's it—that's the ticket!"

"Well, but things are always *there,* aren't they? They were there yesterday and they will be there tomorrow, even if we don't count them. So why count them?"

Humdrum huffed and spluttered and finally said, "Counting keeps you busy! There you go. Work, work. Busy, busy. No time for flying. No time for dreams. Just counting. Watch out for wildebeests but keep counting."

"Watch out for wildebeests?"

"Yes, yes. My Uncle Jabber was counting ants on an anthill. Didn't see a herd of wildebeests coming. Trampled flat."

"Oh dear," said Hodgepodge. "That's horrible."

"Yes, yes. Sad, sad. Watch out for wildebeests, but count. 'Monkey see, monkey count'—that's my motto. There you go. That's the ticket."

Hodgepodge started to ask another question, but Humdrum had climbed up on top of the tree stump and was busy counting the rings. "One, two, three, four, five—"

Hodgepodge left him there. *It would make Mama Moxie and everyone happy if I stopped flying and started counting,* he thought as he walked away. *But counting cannot help me find my first mama.*

After counting the rings on the stump, Humdrum made his way back to the watering hole, muttering, "All hippos are hard-headed, stubborn, difficult, and unreasonable! There you go, that's the ticket."

Humdrum was partially right. There's a fine line between being persistent and being hard-headed, and the more the other creatures tried to talk Hodgepodge out of trying to fly, the more hard-headed he was becoming.

But Humdrum was wrong in saying, "All hippos are hard-headed." After all, he only knew one hippo, namely Hodgepodge.

Nevertheless, Humdrum went around telling the other animals how stubborn and unreasonable all hippos are and the other animals believed him precisely because they had never met any other hippos either.

So all across the savanna, the story spread. Animals who had never thought about hippos before were thinking, "It was a bad day when a hippo came to the savanna. We must make sure no more crazy, hard-headed hippos ever come here!"

CHAPTER SEVENTEEN
HOME OWNERSHIP

"The point is to have adventures, so, those who play it too safe miss the point."
—KRAKATOA THE PARROT-POET

AFTER LEARNING THAT HUMDRUM WAS unsuccessful, Moxie asked Muzzle the old tortoise to talk to Hodgepodge.

"Delighted to share my wisdom!" he said.

Muzzle found Hodgepodge backing away from a large bush, yelling, "Light as a feather! Light as a feather!" Then he ran at the bush and leapt—only to crash down on top of it.

"Ow! Ow!" Hodgepodge said, as he untangled himself from the branches and stickers.

Muzzle shook his head at this odd behavior and croaked, "Hey there, youngster—what do you say we have us a little chat?"

Hodgepodge climbed out of the bush and licked his scratches. *Mama Moxie must have talked to him, too,* he thought.

"Just want to ask you one important question," said Muzzle. "Do you want to live to a hundred and fifty like me?"

"That sounds impossible-old," said Hodgepodge.

"Of course you do," said Muzzle. "But this is a dangerous world, so you've got to protect yourself. You can't be running around jumping off of things and over things and into things all the time. Too risky! Too dangerous! You get my meaning, young fella?"

"I ... I suppose. But—"

"You don't see me jumping off of rocks and tree stumps, do you?"

"Well, no," said Hodgepodge. "But—"

"Of course you don't. I play it safe! I protect myself! That's how I lived to be a hundred and fifty. You see what I mean?"

"Yes, but—"

"Here's what you do, Hodgepodge. Build yourself a nice house."

"A house? I'm not sure that is a thing hippos do."

"No problem. Just use branches and rocks and things you find lying around. Get the monkeys to help. Make yourself a good sturdy house and then you can *stay safe inside your house*. Are you listening to me, young fella?"

"Yes, but—"

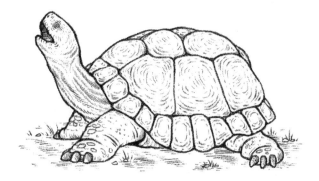

"Here, let me show you." Muzzle pulled his head inside his shell, then called out, "Do you see, Hodgepodge?" His voice echoed. "I'm safe and secure. Comfy and cozy. Home ownership, that's the dream you want. Not this flying foolishness." From inside his shell, Muzzle went on and on about the benefits of home ownership.

Just then, VanDerMugg the rhino came stomping along, not really watching where he was going. With his poor eyesight, VanDerMugg was headed right in Muzzle's direction.

"VanDerMugg, watch out!" Hodgepodge yelled.

VanDerMugg stopped in the nick of time and looked down. "Ah, it's Muzzle," he said. He didn't seem very concerned about almost squashing one of his neighbors.

From inside his shell, Muzzle yelled, "What's that? What's going on?"

"Mr. Muzzle, come out!" yelled Hodgepodge.

Muzzle stuck his head out and looked up to see the rhino standing over him.

"While you were inside your shell trying to stay safe, you almost got trampled," said Hodgepodge.

Muzzle shuffled away, carrying his house with him and grumbling under his breath. "No respect for elders these days."

"Young Hodgepodge. Let's talk," said VanDerMugg.

Oh, maggots, thought Hodgepodge. *What now? Has Mama Moxie ordered all the animals to talk to me?*

CHAPTER EIGHTEEN

"STOMP!"

"Many are frantically chasing success, but real success is not a chase and it's not frantic. Real success is a Wow in the heart."
—KRAKATOA THE PARROT-POET

"**IT'S GOOD THAT I RAN** into you, young Hodgepodge," said VanDerMugg in his deepest, most pompous voice. "Been wanting to give you a little career advice. You do want to be a success, don't you?"

"Success?"

"Yes, success. Success is the key to everything."

"I really just want to learn to fly and find my first mama because I had a dream, you see, and—"

"No, no—flying is not the dream you want. Success is the dream you want, Hodgepodge. It's the only dream that counts. Would you like to know the secret of my great success?"

"Success is a secret?"

"Yes, yes—of course it is."

"Why is it a secret?"

"Why is it a secret? Well, I, uh, that is ... "

"Who made it a secret? Why did they make it a secret?"

"Well, it just is!" VanDerMugg fumed. "And I have discovered the secret. Actually, I've discovered thirty-one secrets to success, but I can boil them all down to one word: Stomp!"

"Excuse me," said Hodgepodge. "Stomp?"

"That's the secret. Stop trying to fly. Learn to stomp!"

"I'm not sure I understand."

"It's simple. Anything that gets in the way of your success, just stomp over it!"

"And that's a secret? Stomp is a secret?"

VanDerMugg ignored this. "Let me give you an example. See those yellow and blue flowers? Imagine that they stand between you and some sweet grass you want to eat. Go stomp over them."

"But Mr. VanDerMugg—they are beautiful. I don't really want to stomp on them. I would rather admire them and smell them. If I want to eat the grass, I could just walk around them."

"No, no—that's not the way to become a success. Listen, it's as easy as one-two-three. One, cultivate poor eyesight like me so you won't worry about what you're stomping on. Two, grow a thick hide like me so no one can hurt you. And three, stomp.

That's all there is to it. Watch." VanDerMugg walked over and trampled all the flowers flat and dead.

"See? That's how you become a success."

"So the secret to success is ... dead flowers?"

"You're missing the point, Hodgepodge! Dead flowers don't matter. What matters is that I'm a success! When you become a big success like me, you can do what you want and no one will question it because, well, because you're a success!"

With that, VanDerMugg stomped away—leaving Hodgepodge to stare at the trampled flowers.

It must be very irritating for VanDerMugg to carry that big horn around on his nose, Hodgepodge thought. *Maybe that's why he is so cranky and confused.*

Meanwhile, the word spread that Muzzle and VanDerMugg had failed to convince Hodgepodge to stop trying to fly. And, as the rumors multiplied—and were often exaggerated—many of the animals were becoming more and more uneasy about having a hippo in their midst.

Strangely, however, the thing that finally sparked The Big Trouble was a chicken. A very scrawny chicken.

CHAPTER NINETEEN
CRASH CHICKEN'S FLYING SCHOOL

"If you need help following your dream, choose your teacher carefully."
—KRAKATOA THE PARROT-POET

THE THREE ANIMALS MOXIE SENT did not persuade Hodgepodge to stop trying to fly, but they did give him an idea—another lumpy, lopsided idea.

Humdrum tried to teach me to count, Hodgepodge thought. *Muzzle tried to teach me to build a house, and VanDerMugg tried to teach me to stomp. Maybe I need someone who can teach me how to fly.*

So Hodgepodge decided that he would look for a flying teacher.

Now it just so happened that on the edge of the savanna there was a village. At the edge of this village there was a hut, and in this hut lived a tribesman who kept a donkey named Genius, a pig named Bubbles, and a bunch of chickens.

One of the chickens was especially skinny and scrawny and the other chickens were constantly making fun of her. They called her Hen and Bones.

"They all think they're better than me," said the scrawny chicken to herself. "But I'll show them. I'll do what no chicken has ever done. I will learn to fly! They'll never make fun of me again."

The scrawny chicken's goal was to fly over Genius the donkey. Every day she would run and flap and flap and take off and crash into Genius's side. And every day the donkey would look around and say, "What?"

For a donkey named Genius, he was no genius.

As the other chickens watched her crash into the donkey every day, they cackled and teased her even more. That's when they started calling her Crash.

Now one day, when Hodgepodge had gone for a long walk, he happened to come to the village and the place where the tribesman lived. And he happened to walk by the barnyard at the moment when Crash was trying to fly over the donkey. He stopped to watch.

Crash ran and flapped her wings and, as she took off, a gust of wind picked her up and carried her over Genius. She crashed in the dirt on the other side.

Crash dusted herself off and clucked. "I did it! I flew!"

Genius said, "What?"

Hodgepodge said, "Wow! Could you teach me how to do that?"

Genius looked at Hodgepodge. "Uh-oh!" he said and ran away. He was getting smarter.

Now if you were a hippo and you wanted to learn how to fly, you would probably not want to choose a chicken for your teacher. Especially a chicken named Crash. But Hodgepodge believed that he and the chicken had something in common: Neither one of them could fly naturally.

That is why Hodgepodge enrolled in Crash Chicken's Flying School.

Genius decided it was safer to stay away from the chickens, so Crash had to find something else to fly over. She told Hodgepodge, "We'll start with something simple: Bubbles's food trough."

Bubbles was a very large, fat, sleepy-looking brown pig with lots of gray spots that resembled bubbles. He spent most of his time either eating or sleeping in the shade. When he heard Crash mention his food trough, he said, "Excuse me, what was that?"

"No worries, Bubbles," said Crash. "We're just going to fly over your food trough."

"I think that is a not good idea," said Bubbles—but he was too lazy to get up and do anything about it.

"Just watch me," Crash said to Hodgepodge. "I'll demonstrate." She started running straight at the food trough, which was full of pig slop. The closer she got to the trough, the harder she flapped her skinny wings.

"She's going to land right in the middle of my dinner," Bubbles said. "I hate it when things land in the middle of my dinner."

But at the last second, inspired by her latest success, Crash flapped and flapped and soared over the food trough—and crashed on the other side.

"See? It's easy!" she said to Hodgepodge. "Now, you try."

"Oh no," said Bubbles. "This is a very not good idea." But he was still too lazy to do anything about it.

"Do you really think I can?" said Hodgepodge.

"Of course you can," said Crash. "Just picture yourself sailing over the trough."

"I can do that," said Hodgepodge. He took off, thundering across the yard, repeating, "I'm sailing over the trough! I'm sailing over the trough!"

"I can't look," said Bubbles. He put his head down and covered his eyes.

"I'm sailing over the trough!" said Hodgepodge. He ran and ran and leapt ... and crashed on top of the food trough, smashing it to bits and spilling slop everywhere.

The tribesman heard the noise and came running out of his hut with his spear. And what did he find? A young hippo lying on top of Bubbles' smashed food trough, covered in slop.

CHAPTER TWENTY
"WHAT JUST HAPPENED?"

"Chaos is the unruly child of fear."
—KRAKATOA THE PARROT-POET

THE TRIBESMAN YELLED AND WAVED his spear at Hodgepodge who jumped to his feet and started running down the main street of the village, trying to get away. When people of the village saw the rampaging hippo, they screamed and scattered in every direction—and this scared Hodgepodge even more and made him run faster.

As the hippo turned a corner at full speed, there was a small girl in the middle of the street, frozen and afraid to move. He swerved to miss her and crashed through a cart full of melons; they went rolling down the street, knocking people over. Several villagers who heard the commotion came running out of their huts and joined the chase, yelling and waving their spears. The terrified hippo kept running and finally broke out of the village with the humans in hot pursuit.

Hodgepodge ran as fast as he could run across the savanna, thinking he could escape. But the tribesmen were very good runners; they followed him all the way home.

With the spear-waving humans not far behind, Hodgepodge came to the watering hole where the animals were gathered. And that's when the watering hole turned into a

complete madhouse, with elephants and zebras and camels and monkeys and gazelles and warthogs bellowing and dashing in every which direction like a disorganized stampede. The air was filled with the roars and trumpets and squeals of the animals and the shouts of the tribesmen—and so much dust was stirred up that nobody could see anything and the animals and humans kept running into each other.

When the dust finally cleared and the noise subsided and the animals had disappeared and the tribesmen had gone home, there was no one left at the watering hole except Hodgepodge.

He sat there in the dusty silence, dazed and confused, wondering, *What just happened?*

And then he had an even more disturbing thought: *What's going to happen?*

CHAPTER TWENTY-ONE
THE BIG TROUBLE

"Our greatest danger is not the stranger but the fear of the stranger."
—KRAKATOA THE PARROT-POET

THE NEXT MORNING, SCAB the camel called an emergency meeting at the watering hole—but he kept it a secret from Moxie. A frightened, angry crowd quickly assembled.

"Hodgepodge is putting us all in danger," Scab began. "He's stirring up the humans, and we all know how dangerous the humans can be when they get angry at animals."

"I agree!" said Clyde the warthog. "We've got to do something and we've got to do it now! What if more hippos show up and start trying to fly? What if there's an invasion of huge, crazy, flying hippos crashing into everything and making the humans mad? It would be a disaster! It would be the end of life as we know it."

All of the animals started talking and yelling at the same time, and the angriest voices were the loudest.

Finally Scab yelled, "Order! Order! Order!" When there was calm, Scab said, "I know many of you tried to reason with Hodgepodge. But let's be honest—it didn't work. Hodgepodge needs something stronger than reason. He needs shock treatment—for his own good, of course. He needs someone who can force him to see the truth. I will volunteer."

"Perhaps you are right, Scab," said Sniff the giraffe. "But I suggest that if your shock treatment does not work, we will have to take action. We simply cannot have someone running around breaking the rules and endangering the whole community."

"Hear, hear," said Clyde the warthog. "If this hippo won't listen to Scab, he should be banished from the savanna and sent back to the jungle where he came from! In fact, banish all hippos!"

Many of the animals began shouting, "Banish all hippos! Banish all hippos! Banish all hippos!"

CHAPTER TWENTY-TWO
SHOCK TREATMENT

"Discouragement is often the gateway to courage."
—KRAKATOA THE PARROT-POET

THAT SAME MORNING, HODGEPODGE HAD awakened with his spirits low and his body bruised and aching. *I don't feel like doing flying practice today*, he thought.

He saw a feather floating on the breeze. The feather fell to the ground and just lay there. Hodgepodge did the same. He lay there.

He was thinking very seriously about giving up on flying.

But then, Scab the camel arrived. He found Hodgepodge lying on the ground next to the feather looking black and bleak, gloomy and glum, deflated and downright discouraged. He looked like a frog that lost its croak or a hummingbird that lost its hum.

Scab, however, didn't notice how low-down and blue Hodgepodge was. You will not be surprised to hear that he was not the most sensitive creature on the savanna.

"Hodgepodge, I'm going to come right to the point," he said gruffly. "You're never going to fly. Not in a million years."

Hodgepodge sat up. Scab sounded quite serious. And a million years sounded like an especially long time.

"You need to face facts, Hodgepodge," Scab continued. "Fact one: You are too heavy. Fact two: You have no wings. Fact three: YOU. WILL. NEVER. NEVER. FLY. You must get that into your head. You must stop this ridiculous quest immediately."

"But Scab ..." Hodgepodge started.

"No more arguments!" Scab said. "If you do not stop this flying nonsense immediately, I am authorized by all of the animals to inform you that you will be banished from the savanna and sent back into the jungle. For your own good, of course. And all hippos will be banished as well."

Hodgepodge looked around. *But I'm the only hippo*, he thought. To Scab he said:

"But my first mama ... "

"Listen, Hodgepodge. Someone has to tell you the truth, and it might as well be me. I take no pleasure in doing it, but I must. I don't think you will ever find your first mother."

"What do you mean?"

"I remember the day Moxie found you and I also remember something that happened in the days before she found you. Some birds told me they had seen hunters in the jungle."

"Hunters?" said Hodgepodge.

"Hunters with spears," said Scab. "Like the ones who chased you here yesterday. I didn't tell you before because I was hoping your mother escaped—but she never came looking for you, so there's really only one conclusion. It's simply a matter of logic."

Hodgepodge said, "You mean she is—"

Scab nodded. "Almost certainly. You need to just forget about her. It's for the best."

"But my mama," Hodgepodge sobbed. "She talked to me! She wants me to find her!"

"That was only a dream, Hodgepodge. And if you want my opinion, dreams are about as valuable as a pile of maggot poop."

"I don't believe you!" Hodgepodge yelled suddenly. "I don't believe you! My dream was real! I *will* find my first mama. I will! I don't believe you!" Then he ran away.

Hodgepodge ran to the watering hole, looking for Mama Moxie. She wasn't there, but all the other animals were. They turned to stare at Hodgepodge and he looked at them. It was like looking at faces of stone. And, suddenly, it hit him:

They don't care about me at all. They just think I'm strange and crazy and dangerous.

He wanted to say something that would make them understand. But when he opened his mouth, all that came out was: "You, you, you ... what I mean is ... I am not ... if you would only ... dreams are ... you are just so ... "

And then, he ran away from the watering hole, too.

CHAPTER TWENTY-THREE
INTO THE JUNGLE

"Running away from your own dark thoughts is like trying to run away from your own shadow."

—KRAKATOA THE PARROT-POET

AT FIRST, HODGEPODGE DIDN'T KNOW where he was running. He just wanted to get away from the stone-faced stares and away from Scab's stinging words. And though he didn't know it, he was also trying to run away from his own dark thoughts.

But running away from your own dark thoughts is like trying to run away from your own shadow. It's very difficult to do—even for a hippo.

Where should he run? The one place where no one would follow him was the jungle, so that's where he went.

As he ran crashing through trees and thick undergrowth,

the branches stung his face—but he didn't notice. Monkeys chattered, but he didn't hear them. Lizards and snakes darted across his path, but he didn't see them.

He ran and ran and ran, deeper into the jungle, until he couldn't run anymore. Finally, he flopped down at the base of a tree and sobbed.

Hodgepodge sat there all alone, all afternoon and into the evening. The night came and there is no darkness quite like the darkness of the jungle at night—and there are also no sounds quite like the sounds of the jungle at night. He heard the squeal of bats, the hiss of snakes, the roar of big cats in the distance, and other sounds he did not recognize.

And he was afraid—so afraid that he sat up late into the night too nervous to sleep until, finally, weariness overcame him.

The next morning, Hodgepodge woke up and looked around.

"Uh-oh," he said.

Every direction looked exactly the same—trees covered with vines. Which direction had he come from? If he wanted to go back to the savanna, which way was the way back?

He had no idea.

"This is not good."

Then, Hodgepodge had an even more disturbing thought. *If I can't go back to Mama Moxie, where can I go?*

All around him there was nothing but deep, dark jungle; in every direction there were animal sounds he didn't recognize. He just sat there, afraid to move.

But then, a blue and red striped lizard dropped out of the tree above, landed in front of Hodgepodge, and hissed at him.

"Aaauuuggghhh!" the hippo yelled. He took off running this way and that like a water bug zigzagging across the water. He crashed over bushes and dashed behind a large tree to hide from the lizard.

He peeked out. No lizard. He took a deep breath.

Then he heard a hiss and looked up. An extremely large boa constrictor was wrapped around a branch directly above him. "Well, hello, delicioussss!" it hissed.

"Aaauuuggghhh!" Hodgepodge took off again, dodging between trees. He wasn't sure how fast a boa constrictor could move, so he ran as fast and as far as he could run until he finally had to stop. His heart was pounding, he was breathing hard, and he looked around nervously. He was afraid the boa constrictor would appear at any moment.

It didn't. Something else did.

A gang of black, angry bats swept down from the top of the trees, squealing and swooping and swarming around Hodgepodge with fiery red eyes and teeth bared for the attack. Frightened out of his mind, Hodgepodge took off running again and kept running until he finally collapsed near a small spring, panting and exhausted.

He had outrun the bats, but what would he find next?

Hodgepodge took a drink from the spring and felt better. But now he was truly, absolutely, completely, totally and thoroughly LOST.

Not knowing what else to do, Hodgepodge sat there by the spring for three days and three nights with only bitter leaves to eat and only his thoughts for company.

And his thoughts were not very good company.

In fact, they were more bitter than the leaves.

On the first day, all of Hodgepodge's thoughts were fearful. Every sound, every sudden movement, every shifting shadow made him jump.

On the second day, his fearful thoughts turned into sad thoughts. *What if Scab is right?* he thought. *What if my first mama really was killed by hunters?*

On the third day, his sad thoughts turned into angry thoughts. He was angry at all the animals for banishing him. He was angry at his dream because of all the problems it had caused. And he was angry at himself for believing the dream. *How could I be so dumb? I'm a hippo, for maggot's sake! How could I ever think that I could fly?*

Finally, he was even angry at his first mother for leaving him alone in the jungle and never coming back to find him.

To put it plainly, Hodgepodge was angry at the whole world.

He woke up on the fourth morning and heard a voice above him.

"Arraakk! May I help you? May I help you?"

CHAPTER TWENTY-FOUR
KRAKATOA

"When times are dark, turn on delight."
—KRAKATOA THE PARROT-POET

HODGEPODGE LOOKED UP. Perched in the tree next to him there was a large, colorful parrot. His head and breast were bright orange and red; his wings were blue, fringed with yellow; his face was white and his beak was black. The parrot stared directly at Hodgepodge with piercing eyes—one eye was green, the other was blue.

"Um ... are you talking to me?" Hodgepodge said.

"Forgive me for intruding," said the parrot. "But I couldn't help noticing that you seem to be one unhappy hunk of down-in-the-dumps hippo."

Hodgepodge didn't really feel like talking to anyone, but he managed to say, "You know about hippos?"

"Do I know about hippos?! At the risk of tooting my own beak and fluffing my own feathers, there's hardly a creature I don't know about. To be perfectly candid, I'm quite an expert in creature features, a professor of flora and fauna. Allow me to introduce myself: Krakatoa, C.F.T."

The parrot fluttered down and landed on a stump near Hodgepodge.

"C.F.T.?" Hodgepodge asked.

"Creature Feature Teacher. So naturally, it's my job to wonder: Why is a young hippo sitting here in the middle of the jungle all by himself looking lower than the mud on a worm's belly?"

"I ... I don't really feel like talking about it," mumbled Hodgepodge. After all he had been through he was, of course, not his usual polite, cheerful self.

"Oh, I see," said Krakatoa. "My apologies—I should have considered that. We don't have to talk about anything really, if you don't want to. We can just sit here and enjoy the beauty of the jungle."

With that, Krakatoa began to whistle a tune and Hodgepodge had no choice but to sit and listen.

After a while, Krakatoa stopped whistling and said, "My grandmother used to tell me, 'When times are dark, turn on delight'." Then he went back to whistling.

This is a strange bird, thought Hodgepodge.

CHAPTER TWENTY-FIVE
SMASHED-DREAM FACE

"Even the best dreams often sound crazy at first."
—KRAKATOA THE PARROT-POET

HODGEPODGE FELT PECULIAR JUST SITTING there while Krakatoa whistled. So finally he said, "I ran away from home."

Krakatoa stopped whistling. "Arraakk! It happens, it happens. I'm sure you had a perfectly good reason plus two or three imperfectly good reasons. And maybe even an atmospheric reason."

"Atmospheric reason?"

"Something in the air. You'd be surprised how many problems that causes. I suppose everybody feels like running away from home once in a while."

"It's actually difficult to explain," Hodgepodge said.

"Isn't it always," said Krakatoa. "Tell you what: To pass the time, let's make a game of it. I'll try to guess why you ran away and you tell me if I'm right or wrong."

Hodgepodge shrugged.

Krakatoa studied Hodgepodge's face. "I'd say ... maybe you lost your best friend? A warthog? A stink bug?"

Hodgepodge thought this was a ridiculous thing to say, but he only answered, "No."

"No? Well, actually, that makes sense," said Krakatoa. "Warthogs and stink bugs make terrible friends. Especially stink bugs. Don't *ever* invite them to a party!"

"I don't actually know any stink bugs," said Hodgepodge. "And I'm not planning any parties. As you can see, I'm lost in the jungle."

"Of course, of course. May I guess again?"

Hodgepodge shrugged again.

"Hmm ... Well, I guess you ran away because you tried telling a joke at the watering hole and even the laughing hyenas didn't laugh—and it was embarrassing."

"I don't know any laughing hyenas, either," said Hodgepodge. "Hippos and hyenas don't get along so well. We certainly don't tell jokes to each other." Hodgepodge thought the parrot should have known this.

"Oh no! Wrong again!" said Krakatoa, flapping his wings. "Okay, one last guess?"

This is an especially strange bird, Hodgepodge thought.

Krakatoa looked directly at Hodgepodge for a while, studying his face. Finally, in a quiet voice, he said, "I guess you had a wonderful dream and you tried to follow the dream, but things didn't work out so well."

Hodgepodge was stunned; he felt like he couldn't speak, could barely breathe. Finally, he managed to mumble, "How ... how did you know that?"

"Comes with my job," said Krakatoa. "To become a Creature Feature Teacher, I had to learn how to read faces. No offense, but you have smashed-dream all over your face."

"I do?"

"Yes—but it's also the face of someone with an interesting story to tell."

"It's not much of a story," mumbled Hodgepodge.

"I beg to differ," said Krakatoa. "I'm sure there is much muchness to your story. Much, much muchness! In fact, I'd bet all my feathers on it. And believe me—you do *not* want to see me without my feathers, mister ... ?"

"I'm Hodgepodge. And you said your name is Cracker ... something?"

Krakatoa chuckled. "Folks often associate us with crackers. Never understood why. My name is pronounced Crack-ah-TOE-ah. So, what's your story?"

"Krakatoa, I don't mean to be rude but, well, I am not really in the mood to talk about it."

"I see. And I suppose you don't want to talk about your dream, either?"

"My dream was stupid," said Hodgepodge. "Mr. Scab the camel said my dream was maggot poop. That made me mad, but now I think he was right."

Krakatoa waved his wings. "Oh, those camels! They're a grumpy, grouchy bunch. They could see the dark side of a rainbow. It probably comes from carrying those huge, heavy humps around on their backs. I suppose that's enough to make anyone grumpy."

"But my dream made me think I could fly over the jungle and find my first mama. Me—a hippo! That's crazy!"

"I wouldn't worry about it," said Krakatoa. "Even the best dreams sound crazy at first. But let me ask you: Why was your mother in the jungle? We don't see many hippos around here."

"I don't really know why," said Hodgepodge. He explained that his first mother left him in the jungle at birth and Moxie the elephant found him.

"My first mama never came back for me," Hodgepodge said. "Then all the animals got upset with me because I kept trying to fly and crashing into things. Then some of the humans chased me back to the watering hole and now the animals think I'm crazy and dangerous—all because of my dream."

"Not to worry. You just got your dream wrong."

Hodgepodge stared at Krakatoa. "I did what?"

"Happens all the time. Most creatures get their dream wrong before they get it right. You have to crack the dream's code."

"The dream's code?"

"Yes." Krakatoa stood up tall and straightened his feathers. "As luck would have it, I am also a Dream Adviser in my spare time. Would you like some help decoding your dream?"

You would think that Hodgepodge would have been thrilled about this possibility but, the truth is, he was torn. On the one hand, he had come to believe that following his dream was a huge mistake and he didn't want to think about it anymore. But, on the other hand, what if the parrot was right? *Maybe I should at least listen to what the strange bird has to say. Besides, it's not like I have anywhere to go or anything else to do*, he thought.

"I guess so," he said.

"Excellent. Tell me all about it."

CHAPTER TWENTY-SIX
THE DREAM'S CODE

"Here's the place to start when you're decoding your dream: Be amazed to be exactly what you are."
—KRAKATOA THE PARROT-POET

THE FRESH MORNING LIGHT filtered down through the tall trees making lacework patterns on the jungle floor. A large yellow butterfly spiraled down through the air as if riding the sunbeams. Behind the young hippo and the colorful parrot, thick jungle vines hung like an immense curtain.

Hodgepodge looked down. Scratching at the ground with his front hoof, he mumbled: "I saw my first mama's face in the moon. Like I said, it was a mad-crazy dream."

"Actually, that kind of thing happens a lot in dreams," said Krakatoa. "A chimp told me she saw her mother's face in a head of cabbage. And a toad said he dreamed about a swarm of flies in the shape of his mother's face."

"Ugh! That's awful," said Hodgepodge.

"Yes—he required a lot of therapy. I mean a LOT of therapy. But let's get back to your dream: What did your mama-in-the-moon say?"

"She told me I'm a hippo. Because, you know, I thought I was an elephant."

"An elephant."

"Yes."

"With a long trunk."

"Yes."

"And big floppy ears."

"I know, I know. That sounds dumb. But I was raised by elephants, and I was quite young when I had the dream."

"No, no—it's not dumb," said Krakatoa. He hopped up onto a branch and started pacing back and forth. "Actually, it's brilliant. And very important."

"I do not see what is brilliant about me thinking I was an elephant."

Krakatoa stopped pacing and looked down at the hippo. "Hodgepodge—when you first learned you were a hippo, how did you feel?"

"I was surprised. I didn't know what a hippo was. But it felt good. Actually, it felt very good."

"You had a Self-Wow moment," said Krakatoa. "In dream decoding that's tremendously important."

"What's a Self-Wow moment?"

"A moment when you're surprised and amazed to be exactly what you are. It doesn't happen often, but when it does—Wow!"

A centipede had crawled out onto the branch with Krakatoa. At this point, she spoke up: "I'm amazed to be exactly what I am."

"And with all those feet, why shouldn't you be?" said Krakatoa

"Want to see me dance?" said the centipede.

"Of course!" said Krakatoa.

Krakatoa whistled a tune and the centipede danced with all of her feet and never stumbled once. It was quite a sight, and Hodgepodge almost smiled in spite of himself.

When the centipede had finished her dance, Krakatoa said to Hodgepodge, "As I was about to say, being amazed to be exactly what you are is the best place to start when you're trying to decode your dream."

"But being exactly what I am has not exactly been all sweet grass and honey," Hodgepodge grumbled.

"That's why we need to talk about the rest of your dream. What else did your mother say?"

"She said: 'Jump into the dream. Save the sunshine. Find the place just right.' I remember because she said it three times."

Krakatoa whistled. "When a dream repeats something

three times, that means it's very, very, very important."

"But she didn't tell me how to find the place just right."

"No problem. The fun is in the finding and the joy is in the journey."

"But what about 'Jump into the dream' and 'Save the sunshine'? None of it makes any sense."

"Of course it does. It makes perfect sense."

"It does?"

"Certainly. We just don't know what the sense is yet. But I have an important question for you: Did your mother say 'Jump into *the* dream?' or did she just say, 'Jump into dream?' Think carefully."

Hodgepodge thought. "I think maybe it was, 'Jump into dream.' But I don't see—"

"Just as I thought. And did she say, 'Save *the* sunshine?' or did she just say, 'Save sunshine?'"

Hodgepodge thought again. "I guess it was, 'Save sunshine.' But what does it matter?"

"In a dream, everything matters. Anything else?"

Hodgepodge hesitated. "Yes—but this is the part that caused all the trouble."

"Can't cook a stew without bubbles; can't follow a dream without troubles," Krakatoa said. "Let's hear it."

"When I asked my first mama how I could get to her, she said: 'Fly like a bird. Fly, fly, fly.' I thought the Wow Spirit would help me fly so I could find her."

"I admit: That is a mysterious clue," said Krakatoa. "But dreams are supposed to be mysterious—that's what makes them so interesting. When we get to the place just right, I'm sure all will come clear. Shall we go?"

"What? Go where?"

"Go find the place just right, of course."

Hodgepodge stammered: "But Krakatoa—I thought we were just talking. I mean ... I appreciate your interest, I do, but that dream has brought me nothing but misery."

"I see," said Krakatoa. "Well, we all have to make our choices, don't we? I do think you would have liked the place just right. It's been wonderful chatting with you, Hodgepodge. Best of luck." Krakatoa stretched his wings, preparing to take off.

"Wait!" said Hodgepodge.

"Yes?"

"You're just going to leave?"

"Hodgepodge, dreams are not about talking. Dreams are about doing. The choice is yours."

"But what if Scab is right? What if my first mama is not even alive? What if there is no place just right?"

"The reason you go on a journey is to find answers to questions like that," said Krakatoa. "One thing's for sure: You'll never find them sitting under this tree."

Hodgepodge stared at the jungle all around him. It was a hard choice, but what else could he do?

He took a deep breath. "Okay."

CHAPTER TWENTY-SEVEN
DEEPER INTO THE JUNGLE

"Be brave or live in a cave."
—KRAKATOA THE PARROT-POET

KRAKATOA TOOK HIS PLACE on top of Hodgepodge's head and said, "Here we go, young Potamus! Take that path to the right."

Why does he call me Potamus? Hodgepodge wondered. He peered down the narrow, densely tangled path. The trees were so close together and covered with vines that very little sunlight reached the ground. The path looked dark and dreary, spooky and gloomy—a path more suited for nasty, dangerous things than for a hippo following a dream.

"Are you sure this is the path to the place just right?" Hodgepodge said, stepping cautiously forward. "Looks more like the path to the place just wrong."

"Arraakk! I feel the Wow, I feel the Wow," said Krakatoa, bobbing his head. "Step lively now! You're moving like a snail crawling through molasses. Be bold or just grow old! Be strong or be wrong! Be brave or live in a cave!"

Hodgepodge mumbled, "There's probably lizards in there."

"What's that?" said Krakatoa.

"Nothing, nothing," said Hodgepodge.

"Wizards? Something about wizards? Or blizzards?"

"No, never mind."

Hodgepodge had heard plenty of stories about the jungle—stories of spotted leopards that could drop silently out of a tree and kill a large animal; stories about wild hyenas that traveled in packs and attacked with razor sharp teeth; and many more.

And of course, he already had experience with a lizard, a boa constrictor, and a gang of bats—so Hodgepodge kept looking nervously left and right as they pushed on through the thick undergrowth.

They didn't see anything dangerous that morning, but they did see toucans with long green beaks and bright yellow breasts, dog-faced baboons, and grinning chimps. They also saw goggle-eyed tree frogs climbing up tree trunks, golden beetles crawling on the ground, and other creatures.

Unfortunately, Hodgepodge was so nervous about what he *might* see that he didn't pay much attention to what he *did* see.

Krakatoa, however, was in a fantastic mood. From his perch on top of Hodgepodge's head, he kept chattering about everything they passed—giving the hippo a guided tour of the creatures of the jungle.

When they came upon some large, hairy, gray-green dog-faced baboons in a tree, the baboons began to cough and bark and smack their lips and shake their heads. They flattened their ears and narrowed their eyes to slits and stuck their tongues out at Hodgepodge and Krakatoa.

"Dog-faced baboons," the parrot whispered. "Bow your head as we go by."

"But they're being very rude," Hodgepodge whispered.

"Just bow your head. I'll explain later."

So Hodgepodge and Krakatoa both bowed respectfully toward the baboons as they passed the tree. The baboons barked and clapped their hands.

Once they were well past the baboons, Krakatoa explained: "A long time ago, some humans in Egypt had a funny idea. They made big statues of a dog-faced baboon and said, 'This is our god!' They bowed down to the dog-faced baboon and worshipped it and brought it expensive gifts. Well, when the dog-faced baboons found out about this, it went straight to their heads. They've been acting like they are the rulers of the universe ever since. And yes—it does make them rude and arrogant and impossible to live with. But the best thing to do is just to humor them and let them go on thinking they are gods so they'll leave you alone. But Hodgepodge?"

"Yes?"

"Don't ever be like them."

Hodgepodge walked on for hours, with Krakatoa commenting on every creature along the path. Occasionally, Krakatoa recited some verses about some of the animals they saw. When a toucan landed in a tree, he said:

*There once was a toucan named Zeke
Who, thanks to his very long beak,
Would fall on his face
All over the place.
Said the toucan: "At least, I'm unique!"*

Hodgepodge rolled his eyes and thought, *the parrot thinks he's funny, but he's not.*

Later in the day, Krakatoa started whistling tunes like a one-bird band. After an hour of whistling, Hodgepodge thought, *doesn't his beak ever get tired?*

Later, with Krakatoa still whistling, Hodgepodge wondered, *does he know all the songs of all the birds in the jungle?*

Still later, he thought, *please, let him stop now. Please, please, please!*

Finally, Hodgepodge couldn't take it any longer. "Excuse me, Krakatoa, but is it absolutely necessary for you to keep whistling like that?"

"Interesting question, Hodgepodge. Is making music necessary? Is it essential? Is it vital and indispensable? Is it—"

Hodgepodge interrupted. "I was not asking for a philosophical discussion. Just a little peace and quiet."

"Yes, a little quiet can be a good thing," said Krakatoa.

"How about a lot of quiet? If a little quiet is good, isn't a lot of quiet even better?"

"That's quite philosophical—for a hippo who doesn't like philosophy."

"Sorry, it was an accident. I'll try not to do it again."

"Ah, an accidental philosopher! I think that must be the opposite of an oriental philosopher. Now that is—"

Just then their conversation was suddenly interrupted.

Whack! Whack! Whack!

"Ow!" yelled Hodgepodge. "Something hit me!"

CHAPTER TWENTY-EIGHT

"NOW I DONE SEEN IT ALL!"

"The jungle's a place where anything can happen. So, that's what you have to be ready for: anything."
—KRAKATOA THE PARROT-POET

WHACK! WHACK! WHACK! WHACK! WHACK!

"Ow! Ow! Ow!" said Hodgepodge. "What the maggot?!" He was jumping and dodging as if a witch doctor had put an evil dancing spell on him.

Looking up, they saw a gang of hairy, orange orangutans high in the trees, screaming and jumping up and down and beating their breasts and throwing down large nuts with their long, hairy arms—and they threw very hard!

Whack! Whack! Whack! Whack!

"Ow! Ow!" said Hodgepodge.

"Run!" said Krakatoa.

Hodgepodge took off running through the trees, but the orangutans followed, swinging and leaping from branch to branch at an amazing speed. And even while they were moving, they grabbed nuts and threw them with remarkable accuracy. (It helped that Hodgepodge was a large target).

Whack! Whack! Whack!

"Ow! They're following us!" Hodgepodge yelled as he ran.

"Faster!" yelled Krakatoa.

Hodgepodge ran faster, but the orangutans kept up.

Whack! Whack!

"They're crazy!" he yelled.

Whack! Whack! Whack!

"But very skillful!" yelled Krakatoa.

Whack!

"Ow! Why do they hate hippos?"

Whack! Whack!

"I don't think they've ever seen one before!"

Now it just so happened that, not far ahead, two old iguanas were sitting high up on a tree branch, chatting like old men on a porch. They were an ugly green, the color of pond scum, and very wrinkled—as if they had been left in the water too long.

"You know, I done seen some crazy, crazy stuff in my life," said the first iguana.

"Yeah, yeah—me too, me too," said the second iguana.

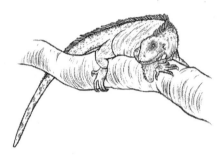

"I seen a warthog so ugly—when he looked in the water to take a drink, the watering hole dried up."

"Naw! It didn't!"

"It did! I swear it did! That watering hole didn't want nothing to do with that warthog or his reflection."

They both cackled.

Just then, the iguanas looked down and saw a hippo with a parrot on top of his head fleeing the deranged orangutans.

"Ow! Ow! Ow! Ow! OW!"

The first iguana watched them go by. "Well, now I done seen it all!"

After some time, the outrageous orange orangutans finally gave up the chase. Hodgepodge stopped to rest.

"What ... what were they?" he said, trying to catch his breath.

"Orangutans," said Krakatoa. "Just having a little fun."

"Fun?! Is that how animals in the jungle have fun?"

"Well, some of them. Sometimes."

"I do not think they understand the idea of fun," said Hodgepodge, still puffing. "Someone should explain it to them."

"How would they explain it?" said Krakatoa.

"Someone should throw nuts at them and ask: 'Do you think this is fun? Are you having fun now?'"

"Interesting idea," said Krakatoa. "Not sure it would work."

"Is someone going to attack us every day—just for fun?"

"No, no—not every day. But the jungle is a place where anything can happen. So that's what you have to be ready for, young Potamus: *anything*."

"Why do you call me Potamus?" said Hodgepodge.

Krakatoa didn't answer.

CHAPTER TWENTY-NINE
A GUIDE'S JOB

"When you're following your dream, never ask, 'Am I there yet?' Just relax and embrace the journey."
—**KRAKATOA THE PARROT-POET**

THE NEXT DAY, ABOUT MIDDAY, they came upon a clearing in the jungle where plenty of long, sweet grass grew.

Hodgepodge stopped. "I'm hungry. Could we get a bite without turning it into a philosophical discussion?"

"Of course," said Krakatoa, bobbing his head. He hopped to the ground and found a seed.

Hodgepodge began gobbling huge mouthfuls of the sweet grass as only a hippo can do. "It's good," he said. "Really good."

He was talking and chewing at the same time, so Krakatoa was treated to the sight of large quantities of half-chewed grass in the hippo's big mouth. Bits of soggy grass flew out in every direction.

The parrot stopped picking at his seed and stared at Hodgepodge.

"What?" said Hodgepodge.

"Oh, nothing," said Krakatoa. He took another tiny bite of seed.

"Were you staring at me?" said Hodgepodge.

"Yes, I was. And I apologize. It is rude to stare."

"What's the matter? Haven't you ever seen a hippo eat before?"

Krakatoa didn't answer.

Hodgepodge took another big mouthful of grass. He chewed loudly and then belched a hippo-sized belch as only a hippo can do: "BRRRRRRAAAAAP!"

"You seem to be enjoying that grass," said Krakatoa.

"I am!" Hodgepodge nodded, chewing again with his mouth open. One bit of chewed grass flew out and hit Krakatoa in his orange breast.

"That grass must taste quite Wow-ish," said Krakatoa, wiping the slobber off with his wing.

"It does."

"So I guess you do believe in the Wow."

Hodgepodge swallowed. He looked at Krakatoa. "I thought we were going to eat without any philosophical discussions. It gives me indigestion."

"Oh, excuse me—I wouldn't want to do that!" said Krakatoa.

"Is that all you're having? One seed?"

"I seem to have lost my appetite."

"Too bad," Hodgepodge said as he took another huge mouthful of grass.

After Hodgepodge had finally finished his meal and topped it off with another hippo-sized burp, he said, "Krakatoa?"

"Yes."

"Why are you doing this?"

"You mean not eating? I eat like a bird."

"No—I mean why are you taking me through the jungle?"

"Ah, that. Professional challenge," Krakatoa said. "You see, I've been a guide and dream advisor to many creatures: a gorilla who dreamed of being a dolphin; a bullfrog who dreamed of being a prince; a depressed zebra who hated stripes; and many others. But this is the first time I've advised a hippo who dreamed of flying."

"Oh."

They continued their journey and it was a long, hot day, and here's what happened: *absolutely nothing.* The only sound Hodgepodge heard was cicadas buzzing. And the only thing he saw was trees, trees and more trees—hour after hour after hour.

The day dragged on and on like a grasshopper with a couple of legs missing and, by late afternoon, Hodgepodge had almost forgotten to feel nervous. Now, all he felt was tired. And bored.

Late in the day, he stopped next to a tree to rest and said, "Krakatoa, how long before we get to the place just right?"

"When you're following your dream, never ask, 'Am I there yet?'" said Krakatoa. "Just relax and embrace the journey."

"But you do have an idea where we're going, right?"

"Not really," Krakatoa said. "That would take the adventure out of it."

"But you're the guide!" said Hodgepodge. "Knowing where we're going and how to get there—isn't that a guide's only job?"

"Sometimes a guide's job is to help you enjoy the journey."

"Excuse me, Krakatoa, but I do not see how I can enjoy the journey when I don't know where I'm going or when I'll get there. It makes no—"

Then he stopped talking. For just at that moment, a large, eight-legged, red and black spider dropped out of the tree and landed on Hodgepodge's snout!

CHAPTER THIRTY
SEVENTEEN DANGEROUS THINGS

"If everyone remembered to be extremely glad to be alive, just think what a world this would be!"

—KRAKATOA THE PARROT-POET

HODGEPODGE'S EYES CROSSED as he tried to look down at the nasty, furry, eight-legged creature on his snout. He found himself face to face with the spider's ugly, gaping mouth and poisonous fangs.

"Careful," whispered Krakatoa in his ear. "It's a redback spider. Very poisonous. It can bite through the thickest hide."

Oh no, oh no, thought Hodgepodge. He felt the spider begin to walk very ... slowly ... across ... his ... snout.

"Be very still," whispered Krakatoa.

Hodgepodge didn't need to be told. He was too scared to move a muscle—too scared to blink. He felt frozen to the spot. In his mind, he counted the spider's steps: *one, two, three, four, five, six, seven, eight.*

The spider opened and closed its mouth and moved its ugly fangs up and down.

Please, please, please spider—just leave me alone, Hodgepodge thought. He squeezed his eyes closed and held his breath.

At that moment Hodgepodge felt something else: Krakatoa's feet inching ever so slowly down from the top of his head, moving carefully between his eyes.

And now the spider was close to Hodgepodge's nose with its tiny, furry feet. The hippo's nose started to tickle. *Don't sneeze! Don't sneeze!* he kept telling himself. *Oh, Wow Spirit—please, please, please.*

And then—

Whap! With a quick movement of his wings, Krakatoa knocked the spider flying. It landed on the ground and scuttled away.

"All clear!" said Krakatoa, fluttering up to a nearby tree branch.

Hodgepodge exploded in a huge, hippo-sized sneeze that scared all the birds away—except Krakatoa, of course. "I almost got killed!" he said.

"But you didn't!" said Krakatoa. "It's an incredible feeling, isn't it? Almost but not quite getting killed? It is ... it is *exhilarating!* Yes, that's the word." Krakatoa paced up and down the tree branch, repeating: "Ex-ZILL-a-rating. Exhila-RATING! I think it is the highest rating you can give an experience."

Hodgepodge stared at Krakatoa as if he had gone crazy. "No! It is not incredible! It is not exhilarating. It is horrible—especially horrible. It's like waiting to get hit by lightning. It's worse than eating live maggots."

"Have you ever eaten live maggots?"

"No, I'm just saying."

"Hodgepodge, look at it this way: A little while ago you were very tired and very bored, right?"

"Yes, but—"

"On a scale of one to ten—where one means feeling dead and ten means feeling extremely, extremely alive—you were probably a two or a three, right?"

"I guess so, but—"

"And how do you feel right now? I'll bet you are an eight or nine at least. Don't you feel extremely glad to be alive?"

"Of course I do, but—"

"Hodgepodge—if everyone remembered to be extremely glad to be alive, just think what a world this would be!"

"You're telling me I should be grateful to the spider for almost killing me?"

"Well, that's not exactly my point, but—"

"Maybe I should look for a pack of hyenas who can almost eat me—just so I can feel glad to be alive again!"

"Interesting idea," said Krakatoa. "But a rather dangerous

one, I think." He hopped back on top of Hodgepodge's head. "Shall we?"

Hodgepodge continued down the path, muttering to himself.

Later in the day, they came upon a fat, lumpy, odd-shaped creature that looked like it was bending over to pray. But then it stood up. It had an extremely long, narrow snout and ears as big as palm leaves.

"That is the most peculiar-looking animal I've ever seen," whispered Hodgepodge. "What is it?"

"An anteater," said Krakatoa. "He's listening to the ground, searching for ants or termites."

The anteater furiously scratched a patch of ground with his front paws and out scrambled dozens of crawling termites, scattering in every direction. The anteater quickly shot out a red tongue twice as long as his long snout and licked up the bugs.

"Yeccchhh!" said Hodgepodge. "He's eating live bugs!"

The anteater turned and looked directly at Hodgepodge. "This variety of termite is actually my favorite. They have a delicate spiciness with hints of sunflower and tree sap. That, combined with a crunchy, woody texture makes them delicious. And, if you don't mind, I would very much like to enjoy my dinner without the extra commentary. Dinner is the high point of my day, you see, and you're spoiling it."

"Oh," said Hodgepodge. "Sorry."

"One more thing," added the anteater. "I may look peculiar, as you say, but at least I belong here. You don't." Then he went back to licking up the termites.

"He's quite touchy, isn't he?" said Hodgepodge as they moved on.

"They can hear very well with those huge ears," Krakatoa explained. "Come on. Let's get some rest."

The travelers found a place for the night. After Krakatoa fell asleep, Hodgepodge lay awake for a long time taking stock of his situation. And the more he thought about his situation, the worse it seemed: *I'm lost. I miss Mama Moxie and Just Bump. I don't know where my first mama is or if she's even alive. I'm following a parrot who doesn't have any idea where we're going. And there must be at least seventeen dangerous things in the jungle that could kill me.*

Just then, Hodgepodge heard the distant roar of a leopard and a chill went through him. *Maybe the anteater is right. Maybe I don't belong here. Maybe this journey is a big mistake.*

CHAPTER THIRTY-ONE
A HIPPO WITH HIS HEAD IN THE CLOUDS

"When you're following your dream, every day matters."
—KRAKATOA THE PARROT-POET

THE NEXT DAY, KRAKATOA was as cheerful as ever, whistling and chattering from his perch on Hodgepodge's head.

As for Hodgepodge, his experiences with the orangutans and the spider had made him as jumpy as a rabbit in a herd of stampeding wildebeests. *At least I haven't seen any lizards,* he thought, looking around nervously.

Just at that moment, they heard a strange shrieking sound coming from above.

AYEEEEEEEEEEE! Smack!

"Ow! Something flew into me!" Hodgepodge said.

Suddenly, the air was full of them—ugly, disgusting, webbed creatures—screaming and hissing and flying all around Hodgepodge—a squealing, squalling storm.

"What are they?" Hodgepodge yelled.

"Flying lizards," said Krakatoa.

"FLYING LIZARDS?! You didn't tell me there were FLYING LIZARDS!"

There were dozens of them: large, wrinkled lizards zooming down from the trees with their webbed legs spread wide. They flew around and around, and some of them crashed into Hodgepodge. Then they scrambled back up a tree and launched themselves into the air again.

"AAAAAAGGGGGGHHHHH!" Hodgepodge yelled. He took off running, trying to get away from the flying lizards, crashing over bushes and dodging through trees until he finally ran full-speed head-on into a large tree and knocked himself completely out.

Hodgepodge remained unconscious the rest of the day and all night, with Krakatoa watching over him. And then, early the next morning—"Arraakk! Wake up! Wake up!"

Hodgepodge opened one eye. Krakatoa was perched on his nose, staring directly at him and bobbing his head.

"Oooowwww!" Hodgepodge groaned, stretching his big hippo body. His head still ached from the collision with the tree.

Krakatoa hopped up on top of his head, which didn't help the headache. "Got to get going if we're going to find the place just right."

Hodgepodge struggled to his feet, still groggy. "It's very hot and my head hurts. Can we take a day off?"

"When you're following your dream, every day matters," said Krakatoa. "Besides, a little walk will help you feel better. On we go!" Then he started whistling.

Hodgepodge moaned and started walking, too groggy to even complain about Krakatoa's whistling.

After several hours, they came to a place where some old trees had fallen over letting the golden sunlight spill down to the jungle floor. And in these bright, sunlit spaces, what did they see? Hundreds of beautiful, delicate orchids of every shape and color imaginable covering the ground like a magic carpet. There were snow-white orchids with delicate pink markings; brilliant maroon orchids with golden markings; orchids as yellow as lemons; orchids as blue as the sky; and others.

"Have you ever seen anything more beautiful?" said Krakatoa.

Hodgepodge mumbled, "Hmph."

A few hours later, they found themselves surrounded by a brilliant blizzard of beautiful butterflies: Dark blue butterflies with yellow spots on their wings; orange and black butterflies;

rich, red butterflies; dainty, pale yellow butterflies; purple and white butterflies; golden butterflies; and others.

"Arraakk! Do you see this? Do you see this?" said Krakatoa, bobbing his head. He was so excited he hopped up and down on Hodgepodge's head. "You can't tell me you don't feel the Wow."

"Oh, I feel something all right," Hodgepodge said. He lifted his aching head only for a moment before he continued on.

The afternoon was very hot and hippos do not do well in the heat. Even so, Hodgepodge trudged on and on—feeling hotter and hotter and more and more tired and more and more miserable until, finally, he stopped.

"I'm going back," he said.

"Excuse me?" said Krakatoa.

Hodgepodge turned around and headed back up the path. "I'm going back to Moxie and Just Bump. You stay here, Krakatoa. The jungle is your home—it's not mine. I don't belong here."

"But what about finding the place just right? What about finding your first mother? What about your dream?"

Hodgepodge kept walking. "It's all maggot poop."

Krakatoa hopped onto Hodgepodge's nose and looked him square in the eyes. "I'll go with you."

"Krakatoa, I want to do this on my own. Please leave."

"But how will you find your way?"

"I don't know. I'll find it. Somehow."

"But Hodgepodge, you'll get lost."

Hodgepodge stopped, suddenly angry. "Krakatoa! You're not listening to me! You're just like all the other grown-up animals. You stand up there all day giving me advice and you don't listen. I didn't really want to go on this stupid journey. And I didn't want to follow my stupid dream, but you talked me into it and it was a really bad-scary idea. I'm going back no matter what you say, so please just LEAVE ME ALONE!"

"Oh," said Krakatoa. "I see. Well, that's ... that's different. But, if you're absolutely sure—"

"YES, YES! I'm absolutely sure!" said Hodgepodge.

Krakatoa sighed. "Okay, if that's what you want."

"It is exactly what I want! Now, go!" Hodgepodge started walking again.

"Be careful. Take good care of yourself," said Krakatoa, hopping to a nearby branch.

"Bye," mumbled Hodgepodge without looking back.

Hodgepodge walked on and on, hour after hour—hotter and hotter and not at all sure where he was going. He walked back past the butterflies and through the field of orchids but he didn't notice them. In fact, he didn't pay attention to much of anything.

"So hot," he mumbled. Things around him started to go fuzzy and blurry. He felt dizzy and the jungle began to spin.

Why does the path keep moving? he thought.

All at once, Hodgepodge fell over and landed with a hard thud that shook the jungle floor. He lay there completely still, unconscious.

High up in a tree nearby, a gigantic boa constrictor watched. He was enormously long and almost as thick as the tree trunk he was wrapped around. "My, my, my," he hissed to himself. "What a magnificent morsel—enough food for half a year!"

The boa constrictor waited to see if the hippo would get back up. When he didn't, the large snake slithered down the tree to the jungle floor, heading in Hodgepodge's direction.

CHAPTER THIRTY-TWO
FINDERS KEEPERS

*"The Dream Advisor's Code:
Never give up on anyone.
For any reason. Ever."*
—**KRAKATOA THE PARROT-POET**

THE BOA CONSTRICTOR REACHED the ground and wove his way toward the unconscious hippo.

"Delicousssss!" he murmured as he slithered up and over Hodgepodge's body toward his head.

"First, I'll wrap myself around his throat. Then, I'll open up my throat." The boa constrictor laughed at his own little joke as he curled his huge, powerful body slowly around Hodgepodge's neck. He had strangled and swallowed a young elephant before, so a young hippo would be no problem.

"Yessss! Yesssss!" hissed the boa constrictor, getting ready to squeeze.

"That's far enough, you legless dirt-eater!"

The boa constrictor looked up to see a brightly colored parrot that had just landed on the hippo's back. It watched him with one green eye and one blue eye. The huge snake laughed, then narrowed his eyes and flicked his tongue at the parrot.

"I'm warning you, parrot. I do not eat often, so I take my dinner seriously," said the snake. "And I do not like to be disturbed when I'm preparing to dine."

"Your brain is no bigger than your legs," said the parrot. "So let me explain the situation clearly: If you release your grip immediately and go away, I will let you live—though, even that is against my better judgment."

"Finders keepers," hissed the boa constrictor. "I found the hippo lying on the ground, so he's mine! Besides—you don't actually suppose you can stop me?"

"Oh, I can't," said the parrot. "But they can." He pointed his beak up toward the trees around them. The boa constrictor looked up and saw a dozen pairs of fierce, orange, beady eyes—the eyes of small, cat-like creatures. They were staring at the snake, making low growls and licking their lips.

A look of fear clouded the boa constrictor's eyes.

"That's right. Mongooses!" said the parrot. "*Hungry* mongooses. If I hear so much as one wheeze from that hippo, one hiccup as a result of your strangling efforts, I will give the word and my mongoose friends will descend on you like starving locusts on a field of grain. They are just begging me to let them do it—for there is enough meat on your slimy body to feed all of their mongoose families for half a year."

The boa constrictor looked up at the trees, then back at the parrot. Reluctantly, he relaxed his grip. "Very well, parrot, you win this round," he said as he slithered quickly away. "But there will be another day." He disappeared into the jungle.

"Thanks gang!" the parrot called out to the mongooses. "I owe you one." They went off, reluctantly, in search of other food.

The parrot—who, of course, was Krakatoa—stared at the unconscious hippo. "What am I going to do with you?" He thought for a while, then he flew away— leaving Hodgepodge on the jungle floor, completely unconscious. And completely alone.

Cicadas hummed. Bats swooped back and forth. A tribe of beetles crawled slowly up and over Hodgepodge's body and continued on their journey. A chimpanzee in a tree watched the hippo for a while, then wandered off to find something to eat.

Finally, Krakatoa returned—accompanied by more than a hundred hummingbirds of all different colors. "Hippos are not good at handling this heat," Krakatoa explained to the hummingbirds. "Help me cool him off."

The hummingbirds zoomed down and hovered just above Hodgepodge's body from head to tail, fanning him with their tiny wings. The soothing sound of a hundred birds humming and the sight of all those birds covering the hippo's body like a rainbow-colored blanket attracted the attention of a gang of monkeys in the trees.

Krakatoa watched Hodgepodge's face and he didn't like what he saw. There was no sign of any consciousness. "Faster, faster!" he said. The hummingbirds stepped up the fanning, bathing the hippo in a cool, refreshing breeze.

"Keep going, keep going!" Krakatoa was getting more worried. But, then, Hodgepodge's head moved ever so slightly. "Keep it up!" yelled the parrot.

Hodgepodge mumbled. One eye flickered open and then the other eye and what did he see? A most amazing sight: more than a hundred hummingbirds of every hue directly above him, fanning his face and body.

"Krakatoa?" said Hodgepodge, weakly. "What's going on? Why are you here?"

"The Dream Advisor's code," said Krakatoa. "Never give up on anyone. For any reason. Ever."

CHAPTER THIRTY-THREE
DREAM ERASERS

"Before you take the safe, easy way, think about all of the adventure you'll miss if you do."
—KRAKATOA THE PARROT-POET

"**WHAT HAPPENED?" HODGEPODGE STRUGGLED** to his feet as the hummingbirds took off.

"Oh, some birds warned me that you might be having problems. I'll tell you about it later," said Krakatoa. "Right now we need to get you some water to drink and I think I know just the place. Not far from here."

At Krakatoa's direction, Hodgepodge left the path and pushed through some thick bushes. It was still very hot and very hard going but, before long, they broke into a clearing and there it was: a beautiful garden much like the one on the savanna where Hodgepodge had his dream. There was plenty of sweet grass to eat and flowering plants sprung up all around—and, yes, even a fresh, bubbling spring.

"Water!" yelled Hodgepodge. He ran to the spring and took a long, long drink.

Krakatoa hopped down and drank as well.

Then Hodgepodge found a patch of sweet grass spiced up with tasty purple flowers. "Mmmmm," he said as he began to devour the grass.

Krakatoa decided he would not watch Hodgepodge eat. Instead, he found some sweet berries on a nearby tree for he, too, was very hungry. He ate one and then—would you believe it?—he even began a second one. That's how hungry he was.

When Hodgepodge had eaten his fill, he burped another hippo-sized burp and looked all around the garden. "What a splendiferous place."

"Yes," said Krakatoa, still nibbling at the second berry.

Hodgepodge closed his eyes. He smelled the sweet aroma of the flowers and listened to the happy, bubbling of the spring. "How delightful it is here!"

"Yes, it is," said Krakatoa.

Hodgepodge opened his eyes. Two dragonflies were zooming around the garden, doing somersaults in mid-air. "I feel good," the hippo said.

"Glad to hear it, glad to hear it," said Krakatoa.

The dragonflies zoomed down and stopped, hovering right

in front of Hodgepodge's face. "I feel spectacularly good!"

"Excellent! Excellent!" said Krakatoa, still eating.

The dragonflies swiveled left, then right, then zoomed off—flying upside down across the garden.

"This is the place just right. I am going to stay here," said Hodgepodge.

Krakatoa said, "Very ... wait, what?" He finally turned to look at Hodgepodge who was sitting in the grass. For the first time, Krakatoa noticed the purple flowers.

"Yes, this is the perfect place," Hodgepodge continued. "This is the place just right. I will stay here and count things the way Humdrum the monkey does. I will start with these delicious little purple flowers. One, two, three ... "

"Hodgepodge, did you eat some of those purple flowers?"

"Yes—and they are especially delicious. I will now eat some more."

"No! Stop!" yelled Krakatoa.

Hodgepodge looked up in surprise.

"Those flowers are called Dream Erasers," said Krakatoa. "They make you forget all your troubles, but they also make you forget about following your dream."

"But they taste so good! I just want to stay here and eat them forever."

"The Dream Erasers are making you think that, Hodgepodge. They are fooling you. Don't eat any more—please!"

But Hodgepodge wasn't listening. He took another big bite of the purple flowers and was starting to chew when they both heard a strange sound in the bushes nearby.

"Hoo-hoo-hoo-hoo-hah-hah-hah!"

Hodgepodge stopped chewing. "Laughing hyenas!" he whispered. "They like to eat hippos."

"The sound was to your right—let's go left," whispered Krakatoa as he flew down and landed on Hodgepodge's head.

Before Hodgepodge could move, they heard, off to the left, "Hoo-hoo-hoo-hah-hah-hah-hah!"

"I'll go forward," whispered Hodgepodge.

But, then, straight ahead they heard, "Hoo-hoo-hoo-hoo-hah-hah-hah!"

"Back, go back," whispered Krakatoa.

But behind them they heard, "Hoo-hoo-hoo-hah-hah-hah-hah."

"Uh oh," whispered Hodgepodge. "We're surrounded!"

CHAPTER THIRTY-FOUR

"HIPPO WITH A SIDE OF POSSUM, YUM!"

"You can't fool all of the hyenas all of the time. But sometimes—"
—KRAKATOA THE PARROT-POET

DARK STORM CLOUDS WERE MOVING in overhead as the hyenas crept closer. Hodgepodge could hear rumbling above and rustling in the bushes all around. *This is very bad. Extremely bad*, he thought.

"Hoo-hoo-hoo-hah-hah-hah-hah. I smell hippo," said a hyena in the bushes in front of them.

"My favorite!" said a hyena to the left.

"Yum—juicy hippo with a side of possum if we can find one. They go so well together," said the hyena in front.

"I claim the eyeballs! I love hippo eyeballs," said a hyena behind them.

"Save the brains for me!" said a hyena to the right.

"There's plenty for all of us," said the hyena in front. "Move carefully, gang. Don't let him get away!"

"Krakatoa!" whispered Hodgepodge. "What should I do? Which way should I run?"

"Lie down," Krakatoa whispered. Then he flew to a nearby tree.

"What?"

"Lie down and close your eyes."

"But you heard them. They want to eat me! They're even talking about side dishes!"

"Lie down and pretend you're dead."

"I won't have to pretend for long," Hodgepodge grumbled.

"Now!"

Reluctantly, Hodgepodge lay down in the grass and closed his eyes. A bumblebee buzzed past his face. He could hear the bubbling spring and smell the sweet flowers, but he could also hear the rustling in the bushes as the hyenas came closer.

Help, Wow Spirit! he thought. *Please, please, please, please, please. I'll never complain again! And I promise to be brave!*

"Is everyone ready to charge?" said one of the hyenas. "Hoo-hoo-hoo-hoo-hah-hah-hah! Altogether now!"

Suddenly, there was a deep growl from the tree where Krakatoa was perched. And then a deep, growly voice said, "This hippo is mine!"

Hodgepodge looked up. Krakatoa winked at him and whispered, "Stay down."

"What the warthog dung was that?" said a hyena behind them.

"A leopard! I'd know a leopard's voice anywhere," said a hyena to the left.

"Where'd the leopard come from?" said a hyena to the right.

"Out of the trees, beetle brain," said the hyena in front. "He beat us to the hippo."

The hyena to the left crept closer and peered through the bushes. "He's right! The hippo is down! The hippo is down!"

"What should we do?" said another hyena.

Using the leopard's voice again, Krakatoa said, "Unless you want to be dessert, I suggest you run away. Fast! Now!"

"Yiyiyiyiyi!" screamed the hyenas, scrambling off through the bushes in every direction, crashing into each other as they went.

Krakatoa waited a few minutes until the sound of escaping hyenas faded into the distance. Then he said, "All clear. Safe to get up now."

"How did you do that?" said Hodgepodge, clambering to his feet.

"It's nothing," said Krakatoa, fluttering down and landing on top of Hodgepodge's head. "It's a little Wow Magic the Wow Spirit gives us parrots. We're good at imitating other creatures' voices."

"It's not nothing—it's amazing!" said Hodgepodge.

"Well, you can't fool all the hyenas all the time, but sometimes you can."

"You saved my life ... again."

"What kind of Dream Advisor would I be if I let you get killed while you're following your dream?"

Hodgepodge thought about all the ways Krakatoa had helped him. "Krakatoa?" he said, "I'm really sorry I said you were like the other grown-up animals. You're not."

"Does that mean you're ready to keep going?"

Hodgepodge looked around at the garden and sighed. "It *is* especially nice here, but I guess it's not a good idea to stay."

"The problem with playing it too safe and easy is that you miss out on the adventure," said Krakatoa, looking up at the dark sky. "And speaking of adventure, here it comes."

CRACK! BOOM! Just at that moment, a bolt of lightning flashed directly overhead, rolling thunder followed, and the rain came in a heavy downpour.

CHAPTER THIRTY-FIVE
DEATH FROM ABOVE

"Trouble is a teacher. It teaches us what we are capable of."
—KRAKATOA THE PARROT-POET

KRAKATOA HUDDLED ON HODGEPODGE'S BACK as they pushed on through the storm, pounded by sheets of rain. The sky had turned so dark that it was hard to see. Trees swayed wildly back and forth as the thunder kept booming and lightning kept flashing, giving them occasional glimpses of the path ahead.

"Krakatoa, are you okay?" Hodgepodge yelled over the sound of the rain.

"Very wet and very fine!" Krakatoa yelled back. "I love a summer rain. Want to hear a summer rain song?"

Hodgepodge grinned. "Why not?"

So Krakatoa whistled his summer rain song.

Finally, in the afternoon, the storm let up. Hodgepodge hoped the rain would at least cool things off but, after it stopped, the heat came back steamier than ever.

And then swarms of mosquitoes attacked. Hodgepodge kept shaking his head and twitching his ears, but the mosquitoes wouldn't go away.

"Right now, it would be very nice to have a shell—like Muzzle the tortoise," Hodgepodge said.

From the top of Hodgepodge's head, Krakatoa began to fan his wings in front of the hippo's face to keep the mosquitoes away.

"Thank you," said Hodgepodge.

Since they were both so occupied with the mosquitoes, neither Hodgepodge nor Krakatoa noticed the big, black vulture circling overhead.

A moment later, they heard a loud screech and looked up; the vulture was diving *at them*.

"Watch out! Take cover!" said Krakatoa as he flew off, trying to get away.

Hodgepodge didn't have to be warned; he was already running to hide behind a big tree covered with hanging vines.

But the vicious, skin-headed bird was not interested in him: It was circling to attack the parrot. Krakatoa knew he couldn't fly fast enough to escape the speedy vulture, so he flew into some thick bushes to hide. Unfortunately, his bright colors made it easy for the big bird to find him.

Hodgepodge peeked out from behind the tree just in time to see some of Krakatoa's feathers fly as the vulture made a direct hit.

"Krakatoa!" he yelled.

Hodgepodge dashed across the clearing. The vulture circled again and went into another dive, but Hodgepodge reached the bush where Krakatoa was hiding a moment before the bird did. He opened his mouth and let out a huge hippo roar that shook the trees—and an amazing thing happened. The vulture screeched and stopped mid-air, turned around, and took off without looking back. It disappeared over the tops of the trees, flying away as fast it could go.

Hodgepodge watched it go, then peered into the bush. There was no sound and no movement. "Krakatoa! Krakatoa!" he said.

Nothing.

Hodgepodge carefully nudged some branches aside with his snout. Deep in the bottom of the bush, he saw some color. He nosed more branches out of the way and there was Krakatoa's body—limp, still, eyes closed.

"Krakatoa!" he cried.

Silence. No movement. Not even a wiggle.

"Krakatoa! Say something."

Nothing.

"Oh no, oh no, oh no," moaned. "Krakatoa—you can't be dead. I need you. How am I going to find the place just right or find my first mama without you?"

Krakatoa lay there like a wrung-out colored rag as Hodgepodge nudged him with his snout. Huge hippo tears rolled down his cheeks and washed over Krakatoa's limp body.

"Krakatoa!" he moaned. He closed his eyes and sobbed for quite some time, repeating Krakatoa's name over and over and bathing the parrot's body with his tears.

It was no use. After a long time, Hodgepodge finally lifted his head out of the bush, heaved a heavy sigh, and started slowly down the path. Alone.

CHAPTER THIRTY-SIX

AN ESPECIALLY BIG HEAD

"There's only one way to be in the world without any troubles—and here it is."
—KRAKATOA THE PARROT-POET
(LOOKING AT A SKELETON)

WHAT DO I DO NOW? Hodgepodge wondered as he walked away. But then, he thought he heard a faint sound. He turned around and listened.

Nothing.

"Just my imagination," he muttered and turned to go.

Then, he heard it again. He stopped and looked around. Yes, there it was—a faint whistle.

Hodgepodge rushed back to the bush and looked in. "Krakatoa? Is that you?"

Now he could definitely hear a weak whistle coming from deep inside the bush. Hodgepodge nudged the branches aside until he could see Krakatoa's limp body.

"Krakatoa! Krakatoa!"

Krakatoa's green eye opened, then his blue eye. He looked up to see Hodgepodge's huge head, poking into the bush right in front of his beak.

"Has anyone ever told you that you have an especially big head?" said Krakatoa.

"Krakatoa! You're alive!"

"Apparently. Is the vulture gone?"

"Yes! Are you okay?"

Krakatoa checked his wings and feathers. "Thanks to you, I've still got most of my feathers."

"It was going to kill you!" said Hodgepodge.

"Yes, I believe that was the plan," said Krakatoa.

"But you're okay? Are you sure you're okay?"

Krakatoa managed to flutter up and take his place on top of Hodgepodge's head. "I'm fine, I think. I'll just rest up here for a while if you don't mind."

"Mind? No, I don't mind. Of course I don't mind," said Hodgepodge.

"By the way, that was some roar," said Krakatoa. "I heard it just before I passed out. It must take a big head to roar like that."

Hodgepodge grinned. "I didn't know I could do that. Is that a thing hippos do?"

"Yes—and you picked a good time to find out."

With Krakatoa on top of his head, Hodgepodge continued. He walked slowly and carefully to protect the parrot.

Before they had gone very far, they came across a skeleton.

Hodgepodge stopped. He was afraid to ask.

"It's not a hippo," said Krakatoa. "It's a hyena skeleton. Maybe the vulture had laughing hyena for dinner and wanted me for dessert."

Hodgepodge stared at the skeleton. "No more laughing for him."

"No more troubles either," said Krakatoa. "Hodgepodge, there's only one way to be in the world without any troubles—and here it is."

As they stood there, staring at the skeleton, Krakatoa said, "Hodgepodge? Thank you."

CHAPTER THIRTY-SEVEN

AN EDUCATION FOR FASCINATION

"The Wow is always there inside you even when you don't feel it. You just have to learn to listen to it."

—KRAKATOA THE PARROT-POET

AFTER THE HYENA SKELETON, our travelers found a place to spend the night.

Hodgepodge made himself a bed of leaves and Krakatoa found a branch to perch on, safe from ground predators.

The night was very dark but, after a while, there was a break in the clouds and the full moon appeared between the trees—large and luminous, shimmering and silvery, mysterious and magical.

"I wish I could swallow the moon," said Hodgepodge.

"You must be very hungry," said Krakatoa.

"No—but if I swallowed the moon, I would have all that light inside to help me when I'm feeling dark."

"Hmm."

"I hope my first mama is looking up at this moon right now."

"Wherever she is, I'm sure she loves you. And I think she must be full of Wow."

Hodgepodge thought about this. "I do not think I have a large amount of Wow in me. I am still afraid of lizards."

"You saved me from the vultures! That was very Wow-ish. And look at all the dangers you've survived. It took some Wow just to go on this journey."

"I do not feel very Wow-ish."

"Hodgepodge, listen to me," said Krakatoa. "The Wow is like the moon. Sometimes the moon is full, sometimes it looks like it's only half there and sometimes it seems to disappear—but the moon is always there even when we don't see it. And the Wow is always there inside you even when you don't feel it. You just have to learn to listen to it."

"Krakatoa? Can you teach me how to listen to the Wow inside me?"

"Now *that* is an education for fascination. That is a school for no fools—a course of a different color. Are you sure you're ready?"

"I don't know," said Hodgepodge. "I hope so."

Krakatoa stood up tall and straightened his feathers. "Okay, lesson number one. Repeat after me: I am Hodgepodge, the one-and-only me."

"I am Hodgepodge, the one-and-only me."

"Now say: I am Hodgepodge and there is no one like me."

"I am Hodgepodge and there is no one like me."

"Now say: I am Hodgepodge—and no matter what has happened or what anyone says—I am a good thing."

Hodgepodge hesitated, then said, "I am Hodgepodge—and no matter what has happened or what anyone says ... " he trailed off. "I can't say it."

"Is the moon a good thing?" Krakatoa asked.

"Yes."

Some fireflies were fluttering around them, lighting up the night. Krakatoa said, "Are the fireflies good things?"

"Yes." Hodgepodge smiled.

"Then you are, too. Now go ahead and say it, please."

"I am Hodgepodge—and no matter what has happened or what anyone says, I am a good thing."

"Arraakk! End of lesson one, end of lesson one."

CHAPTER THIRTY-EIGHT
HIPPO-CRITICAL

"If you ignore those who are hippo-critical, they have no power to hurt you."
—KRAKATOA THE PARROT-POET

THE NEXT DAY, HODGEPODGE was quiet as they continued on their journey.

Krakatoa leaned over the top of his head and looked him in the eyes upside down. "Thinking about something?"

Hodgepodge *was* thinking about something. He was thinking about lesson number one. "The other animals on the savanna do not think I am a good thing. They think I'm crazy."

"Ah, well, we're all a little crazy at times," said Krakatoa. "You should see my Uncle Vesuvius. He speaks five languages and nobody understands any of them."

"But they called me the hysterical hippo and the fat splat. And now—if I went back to the savanna and told them I've been going through the jungle with a parrot on my head, there's no telling what they might call me."

"Maybe bird-on-the-brain?" Krakatoa said. He fluttered to a nearby branch so he could look at Hodgepodge right side up. "Hodgepodge, I'm sure some of the animals on the savanna had good intentions, but there were two things they didn't understand."

"What two things?"

"First, they didn't understand your dream. And why should they? It is your dream—not theirs. You wouldn't understand a hummingbird's dream."

"I didn't even understand my own dream," said Hodgepodge.

"There you go," said Krakatoa. "Dreams are not easy to understand."

"What is the second thing they didn't understand?"

"You."

"Me?"

"Yes. They had never seen a hippo before. And, unfortunately, sometimes when folks meet someone who is different, they just criticize. They were hippo-critical! But you have a secret power over hippo-criticalness."

"I do?"

"Ignore it—ignore, ignore, ignore. Ignore all quislings and quibblers. Ignore all nattering nitpickers, all petty pettifoggers and carping critics and flimsy faultfinders. If you ignore those who are hippo-critical, they have no power to hurt you."

"I guess that's another Wow lesson, right?"

"You guessed correctly, young Potamus."

CHAPTER THIRTY-NINE
THE ANSWER AFFLICTION

"A question a day keeps the boredom away."
—KRAKATOA THE PARROT-POET

THE NEXT DAY, A GECKO darted across the path. It made Hodgepodge jump, but it quickly disappeared under a bush.

"You okay?" said Krakatoa.

"I saw a lizard," said Hodgepodge. "But it's gone."

"It was a gecko," said Krakatoa, reciting the following verse:

The gecko, a lizard with class,
Can climb up the slipperiest glass.
He can be so tricky
'Cause his toes are so sticky,
But I'll bet his socks are a mess!

Hodgepodge laughed. Later, when they saw a magpie, Krakatoa recited:

When a magpie is hungry, she'll munch
On other birds' eggs by the bunch.
And though she complains,
I think this explains
Why she's never invited to lunch!

"Why are you always making up verses?" Hodgepodge asked.

"As a way of keeping up one's spirits, it's easier than swallowing the moon. And besides, the world is here for our enjoyment. See those chimps?"

Two chimps were chatting in a tree. Hodgepodge and Krakatoa stopped to listen.

"Would you bug me?" said the first chimp.

"But it's your turn to bug me!" said the second chimp.

"No—I bugged you yesterday. It's your turn to bug me!"

"All right. I'll bug you first if you'll bug me after."

The second chimp started picking bugs out of the first chimp's fur while the first chimp sighed with pleasure. "That feels soooo gooooood!" he said. "I love it when you bug me."

Hodgepodge laughed as they continued. Then he said, "Speaking of bugs, there's a question that's bugging my brain."

"A question a day keeps the boredom away. Let's hear it."

"Why would the Wow Spirit send me a dream that made me *think* I could learn to fly? Because, of course, I can't."

"Excellent question!" said Krakatoa. "An A-1, premium

grade, first-prize question. My professional advice is this: Hang on to that question."

"You don't have an answer?"

"Answers are highly over-rated. I'd rather have one really good question to chew on than a camel's hump full of answers."

"But Krakatoa—the point of asking a question is to get an answer!"

"Not always," said Krakatoa. "Sometimes the point of asking a good question is to stir up your brain so you can hear the Wow. Remember Hodgepodge: A good question will lead you on an exciting quest—if you are willing to go where it leads."

Hodgepodge stopped. "When I was very small, I loved questions. I asked them all the time."

"Never too late to love them again! And here's another good reason to love the questions: They will help you avoid the dreaded Answer Affliction."

"Answer Affliction?"

"The Answer Affliction is a terrible disease; it strikes those who think they have all the answers."

"I think some of the animals on the savanna had the Answer Affliction."

"Could be. The Answer Affliction causes hardening of the head and hardening of the heart. The ones who have it are so busy pretending they have all the answers that they forget to love the questions or go on the quest. They are like someone who studies a map and then boasts about the great journey they took."

"I suspect a Wow lesson is coming," said Hodgepodge.

"You suspect right," nodded Krakatoa. "Love the questions. And love the quest. And don't forget to enjoy the world!"

Just then, they heard a tiny voice above. "Coming in for a landing!"

CHAPTER FORTY
THE FLYING SPIDER'S TALE

"When you rise above your fears, you're free!"
—KRAKATOA THE PARROT-POET

THEY LOOKED UP AND SAW a black and yellow spider sailing down through the air.

"A flying spider?" said Hodgepodge.

"Yes, indeed!" said Krakatoa.

"Is he poisonous?"

"No, no. Not at all."

The spider made three slow, wide circles and landed softly on a tree leaf near Hodgepodge.

"Most impressive," said Krakatoa. "This is Hodgepodge and I'm Krakatoa."

"Chance, the flying spider," he said. "Just flew in from Madagascar."

"Amazing," said Hodgepodge. "You fly without wings?"

"Why is everyone so interested in wings?" said Chance. "That's old technology! We spiders have something much more advanced: Silver threads. Permit me to demonstrate."

Chance held up one of his eight legs to test the breeze. He closed his eyes, hummed and, suddenly, three long silver threads shot up into the air and combined to catch the breeze like a kite on a string.

"Tally ho—off I go!" said Chance as the breeze lifted the silk kite along with him up, up, up into the air. "No wings and no effort! Just riding the breeze!" he yelled. "A more civilized way to travel, if you ask me." He flew around in a circle, then floated gently back down.

"Splendiferous!" said Hodgepodge. "How did you learn to do that?'

"Excellent question," said Chance. "And an excellent question deserves an excellent story. Fortunately, I have just such a story and it happens to be the story of my life. Would you like to hear it?"

"Yes, please," said Hodgepodge.

"When I was young, I noticed that there were two kinds of grown-up spiders: food spiders and flying spiders. Food spiders *only* use their silver threads to make webs for catching food. But flying spiders are different. They do make webs to catch food, but most of the time, they use their silver threads to fly.

"Well, as I grew, the time came for me to choose which kind of spider I wanted to be and, let me tell you, it was not an easy choice. Flying sounded exciting, but it was also dangerous. I had heard stories of flying spiders that were swept away by storms or eaten by birds.

"On the other hand, the life of a food spider is safe, easy and comfortable. They always have plenty to eat—and we spiders do love to eat! In fact, many of my friends were choosing to be food spiders and that made my choice even more difficult.

"But I noticed something. Whenever I listened to flying spiders tell stories about their travels and adventures, I heard an excitement in their voices and saw a spark in their eyes. Food spiders didn't tell stories. They would say things like: 'Flying is dangerous!' or 'Will flying put food on the table?' And even though they made sense, there was no spark in their eyes.

"I thought long and hard, but I finally made my choice. One day, I shot out my first three silver threads. The breeze lifted me up and I flew and, at first, I was terrified! But then, I began to look around. I looked at the jungle below, I looked at the sky above and, in that moment, I understood."

"What did you understand?" said Hodgepodge.

"I understood that flying is really about rising above your fears."

"And when you rise above your fears, you're free!" said Krakatoa. "Bravo!"

"Couldn't have said it better myself," said Chance.

"Thank you for your story," said Hodgepodge.

"Well, I must be going. More adventures await!" He took off, yelling, "Tally ho!" as he sailed up above the trees and out of sight.

CHAPTER FORTY-ONE
THE BEST KIND OF WOW MAGIC

"Here's the test to see if you're listening to the Wow: Is there a spark in your eye? Is there a spring in your step? Is there a song in your heart?"
—KRAKATOA THE PARROT-POET

AS THEY CONTINUED, HODGEPODGE GRINNED and said, "Even if I *could* make silver threads, it would take about a million threads to get me up into the air."

Krakatoa bobbed his head. "A hippo floating across the sky held up by a million silver threads—that would be a sight to see!"

"Krakatoa, you said I have to crack the code to understand my dream, right?"

"Yes."

"When Chance the spider said that flying is really about rising above your fears, that reminded me of something in my dream. Something I forgot until now."

"Oh, I can't wait to hear this!"

"Just before my first mama told me to 'fly like a bird,' she said: 'Be brave; don't let fear hold you down.' Maybe 'fly like a bird' was code for, 'Rise above your fears.' Do you think that is right?"

"It's your dream. Do *you* think it is right?"

"I think so," said Hodgepodge. "I do *want* to be brave. When I find my first mama, I want her to see a spark in my eye."

"An excellent thing to want," said Krakatoa. "My grandfather used to say, 'Here's the test to see if you're listening to the Wow: Is there a spark in your eye? Is there a spring in your step? Is there a song in your heart?'"

"That is definitely a Wow lesson," said Hodgepodge.

"Yes, yes," Krakatoa said, bobbing his head. "It's the best kind of Wow Magic."

CHAPTER FORTY-TWO

BULL

"Every living thing has a story."
—**KRAKATOA THE PARROT-POET**

ON THE SAME DAY that Hodgepodge and Krakatoa were listening to Chance's story in the jungle, there was a sad, solemn gathering of hippos far away on the bank of the wide river.

Bull, the old hippo—the magnificent leader and protector and the only male of the tribe—had died.

There were many hippo tears, of course, and some of the hippos shared stories about the great things Bull had done when he was young and strong.

One of the older female hippos told about the great flood that happened when she was a child. "I was out in the middle of the river when a raging wall of water suddenly came sweeping down," she said. "The river was so powerful that it was uprooting small trees along the bank and carrying them away. So when the wave hit me, there was nothing I could do and no one could reach me. No one except Bull. He didn't hesitate—he ran into the middle of that powerful, raging river, grabbed me by the back of my neck, and pulled me safely to the bank where I was reunited with my frantic mother."

Another hippo remembered the times when she would go to sleep to the sound of Bull's thunderous roars as he cruised up and down the river, scaring the crocodiles away. "I remember how comforting it was to hear Bull roaring at night," she said. "That sound told me we were safe."

Still another hippo remembered when Bull fought three crocodiles at once. "He saw them sneaking up on some of our children," she said. "He went charging out to meet them. I thought the three crocs were going to be too powerful for him and, apparently, the crocs thought the same thing. Instead of fleeing, they decided to fight him. It was the last fight of their life."

After these and other stories, the oldest hippo, Glory, spoke: "We are all grateful for the life of Bull, a magnificent hippo who was our fearless leader and protector. He was full of Wow. Let us honor Bull's memory by being strong and brave and by fighting the crocodiles as best we can—so we can live in peace in this beautiful place."

But the thought in every hippo's mind was, *what will happen to us now?*

On the far bank, two crocodiles were watching from a distance.

"Terrible about the hippos losing their leader," said the first croc.

"So sad. My heart is about to break," said the second croc as two crocodile tears trickled down his face.

"What will we do without him?" said the first croc.

"Oh, I can think of a few things," said the second croc, grinning and licking his ugly lips.

CHAPTER FORTY-THREE

A ROAR OF BRAVERY AND JOY

"The cure for asking 'What if? What if?' is to ask, 'What now?' and live all day as if right now is all that matters."
—KRAKATOA THE PARROT-POET

BACK IN THE JUNGLE, several days went by when absolutely nothing happened—just more walking and more cicadas buzzing and more vine-covered trees. As they walked, Hodgepodge told Krakatoa the whole story of his life while Krakatoa asked many questions and shared many observations.

Eventually, however, Hodgepodge ran out of stories to tell and time began to drag. He was in a much better mood than before, of course, but he found himself almost wishing for the days when they were chased by orangutans. At least, then, there was some excitement.

One long day, Hodgepodge said, "Krakatoa? We have been in the jungle a very long time."

"True."

"I am just thinking … what if we never find the place just right? What if I never find my first mama or any other hippos? What would I do then?"

"Sounds like you've got a bad case of the 'What-ifs,'" said Krakatoa. "Just a whiff of the 'What-ifs' can give your dream the sniffles. Fortunately, there is a cure."

"And I'm sure you will tell me what it is."

"The cure for asking 'What if? What if?' is to ask, 'What now?' and live all day as if right now is all that matters." Then Krakatoa recited:

Here and now, here and now,
The place and time to find your Wow;
And when you find your Wow in the now,
You'll be the master of What and How.

Well, there's nothing much happening here and now, Hodgepodge thought. So he decided he would make use of the time to practice his roar.

He tried a soft roar, then a loud roar. He tried a low roar and a high roar. He tried short roars and long roars. As he went roaring through the jungle, monkeys screeched and scampered to the tops of trees, birds took off for the heavens, and even snakes slithered quickly away.

"Uh ... Hodgepodge?" said Krakatoa.

"Yes?"

"I know you're proud of your roar—as well you should be—but we don't want to frighten every creature in the jungle."

"Oh, yes, I understand," said Hodgepodge. "I shall save my roar for special occasions. But Krakatoa, what did you think of it? Is it a good roar?"

"Honestly, I think it is an excellent roar."

"I was going for a roar that is sort of a combination of bravery and joy—but I wasn't sure that came through."

"I think bravery and joy came through just fine."

At that moment, they saw a yellow lizard crawling head-first down a tree in front of them. The lizard froze, its bulging eyes on Hodgepodge and its tongue flicking in and out. Hodgepodge froze too. They stared at each other.

"Krakatoa?" Hodgepodge whispered.

"Yes?"

"Do you think it would be all right if I used the roar one more time?"

"Arraakk! Be my guest, be my guest."

Hodgepodge took a deep breath and roared his best roar. Instantly, the yellow lizard shot straight up to the top of the tree as fast as lightning—backward!

Hodgepodge laughed. "Did you see that? Backward—all the way to the top! How did he do that?"

"It looked like an invisible giant yanked him up by the tail," said Krakatoa.

They laughed, and then, as Hodgepodge resumed walking, Krakatoa said, "Sooooo ... I guess this means you're over the lizard thing?"

Hodgepodge grinned. "I guess so."

The hippo stopped. Blocking the path in front of them was the largest, fiercest lizard Hodgepodge had ever seen—a lizard as large as a wild boar. He was black with red beady eyes. He pawed the ground, snorted angrily, and stared at Hodgepodge with a look of pure evil.

Hodgepodge whispered, "Or maybe not."

CHAPTER FORTY-FOUR
DRAGON

*"Here and now, here and now,
The place and time to find your Wow;
And when you find your Wow in the now,
You'll be the master of What and How."*
—KRAKATOA THE PARROT-POET

THAT IS A BIG LIZARD," said Hodgepodge.

"Komodo dragon," said Krakatoa. "The largest and meanest of lizards."

The Komodo dragon had planted his powerful legs firmly in the middle of the path as if he had no intention of moving. The trees and undergrowth were very thick on either side of the path making it impossible to go around him.

"Let's turn around," whispered Krakatoa. "Maybe you can outrun him."

"Maybe?" said Hodgepodge.

The Komodo dragon hissed.

Hodgepodge turned around and started back down the path. But, after he had taken a few steps, he stopped.

"He's starting to follow," whispered Krakatoa. "Keep going!"

Hodgepodge turned back to face the big lizard. The Komodo dragon stopped and hissed again.

"Hodgepodge, what are you—"

"Krakatoa, please find a tree branch," Hodgepodge whispered.

"But this is not a normal lizard," whispered Krakatoa. "It is the crankiest kind of lizard. And the largest. And the strongest. And the most vicious."

"If you are trying to encourage me, you are doing a bad job."

"But Hodgepodge—"

"Please, Krakatoa. I must do this. I must do this by myself."

The Komodo dragon bared his teeth and hissed again.

"Are you sure?"

"Yes," said Hodgepodge. "I am especially sure. Please."

Krakatoa flew up to a nearby tree to watch.

Hodgepodge stared at the Komodo dragon, whispering to himself, "Here and now, here and now." Then he took a deep breath and called out: "Excuse me, but you are blocking our path. I'm sure this is not intentional on your part—so if you would please let us by, there will be no trouble."

The Komodo dragon laughed. "Oh, there's going to be trouble, pal," he said and took a step toward Hodgepodge. "There's going to be a lot of trouble and a lot of hurt."

Hodgepodge gulped. Then he took another deep breath and roared a long, loud roar. Trees shook and birds scattered.

The Komodo dragon stared at Hodgepodge. "That's it? That's all you've got?"

"If you don't let us by, I shall have to roar again!" said Hodgepodge.

"You want me to run away just because you made a pathetic noise? You're out of touch with reality, pal. You do not understand what is going down here."

"The reality is simple," said Hodgepodge. "We need to go on this path. You are blocking the path. And so I will ask you again to let us go by."

Watching from a tree branch, Krakatoa called down, "Hodgepodge, I'm not sure this is a good idea."

"You're not helping!" Hodgepodge whispered back, keeping his eyes on the big lizard.

"Let me tell you what reality is, you fat lump of flabby hippo meat," said the Komodo dragon. "I'm going to come over there and grab you by your fat hippo throat. Then, I'm going to chomp down very hard on your fat hippo throat and hold on very tight for a very long time. And then you will die. And then I will bring all of my family and we will feast for days on your fat, juicy hippo meat. *That* is reality. *That* is what's going down."

Hodgepodge gulped and then roared again, even louder. The ground shook.

The Komodo dragon stared at Hodgepodge as if he were crazy.

Then—all at once—the huge lizard charged with surprising speed and threw himself at Hodgepodge, locking his jaws on the hippo's throat. Hodgepodge roared in pain. He shook with all his might, again and again, and finally shook the lizard off. The Komodo dragon went flying and immediately scrambled back up.

Hodgepodge roared again and charged, colliding with the Komodo dragon. The two of them went rolling on the ground. Monkeys in the trees watched the battle, cheering and jumping up and down.

Hodgepodge tried to pin down the Komodo dragon, but the big lizard was very quick. He scrambled away, backed off, and charged again. This time, Hodgepodge head-butted the lizard, knocking him onto his back. The Komodo dragon jumped up, backed away and shook his head. He charged again.

At the last split-second, Hodgepodge dodged so that the

Komodo dragon crashed headfirst into a big tree. Stunned, the big lizard slowly got to his feet. But before he could attack again, Hodgepodge chomped down on the Komodo dragon's flailing tail.

Eeeuuuwww! Hodgepodge thought. *His tail smells like camel dung.* He held on to the slimy, thrashing, foul-smelling tail as the Komodo dragon fought with all his might to get away.

Then, the hippo lifted the huge, wriggling lizard up by his tail and whirled him around and around in circles, faster and faster and faster and finally threw the Komodo dragon way off into the jungle, whirling and screaming. The lizard crashed in the bushes and ran away screeching.

Hodgepodge yelled after the retreating beast: "I'm not fat! I'm mostly muscle!"

Krakatoa fluttered down to join Hodgepodge. "Are you okay?"

Hodgepodge breathed hard. "I didn't run away." He sounded surprised at himself.

"You certainly didn't!" said Krakatoa. "You were amazing."

"Krakatoa? This fighting thing. Is this another thing hippos do?"

"When necessary," said Krakatoa. "When necessary."

"I have never seen such a lizard. In his way, he was very Wow-ish. I suppose I should thank him."

"Really? Why?"

"He helped me to finally get over my fear of lizards ... I think."

"Ah," said Krakatoa, as he hopped back onto the top of Hodgepodge's head. "That's good."

As Hodgepodge walked away, he let out one more, mighty roar that echoed throughout the jungle. Then he looked up to the sky and yelled, "I AM HODGEPODGE, THE ONE-AND-ONLY ME!"

Monkeys in the trees chattered and cheered.

Then he yelled: "I AM HODGEPODGE AND I AM GLAD TO BE ALIVE!"

The monkeys cheered again.

Finally, he yelled, "I AM HODGEPODGE AND I AM A GOOD THING!"

"Well done, Hodgepodge," said Krakatoa.

"I did the 'here and now' thing," said Hodgepodge. "Did you hear me do the 'here and now' thing?"

"Arraakk! I did, I did." Krakatoa bobbed his head up and down.

"I think I found my Wow in the now. Do you think I found my Wow in the now?"

Krakatoa bobbed his head up and down again. "Definitely."

I wish Mama Moxie and Just Bump could have seen me today, Hodgepodge thought as they continued on their way. *And I wish my first mama could have seen me.*

CHAPTER FORTY-FIVE
SHADOW'S STORY

"Is life a painful problem or is it a precious, priceless gift? The answer is: Yes."
—KRAKATOA THE PARROT-POET

AS THEY CONTINUED, THEY FOUND themselves again in the middle of another brilliant blizzard of beautiful butterflies of every color and design.

Hodgepodge turned in circles to admire them; the butterflies surrounded him, fluttering happily around his eyes and ears and landing on his head. One even landed on his nose.

"Stupendous! Marvelous! Splendiferous!" said Hodgepodge. "The words are not enough. We need new words!"

Krakatoa said, "Flutterific!"

Hodgepodge added, "Happy-magical!"

Just then a tiny, squeaky voice said, "Watch out world—here I come!"

Hodgepodge looked up. On a low branch just above his head, a baby bird was perched on the edge of a nest. It squeaked, "Yippee!" then leapt off and fell straight down, flapping its stubby wings all the way and landing with a small bounce on the ground.

"Ouch!" it squeaked. It flapped its stubby wings some more, trying to get off the ground—but it only managed to elevate a couple of inches before it fell back.

"Uh-oh," it squeaked. "Not good."

"That was a brave try, little guy," said Hodgepodge remembering his own attempts at flight. "I don't think you're quite ready for flying yet."

The baby bird looked up at the hippo. "My mother is going to be quite displeased with me."

"I'll help you back up." Hodgepodge lowered his head to the little bird. "Climb up on my snout." The baby bird climbed on and Hodgepodge lifted him back up to the nest.

"Just be patient, little guy," said Hodgepodge. "You'll be flying soon."

"Okay," squeaked the baby bird. "Thank you!"

Just then, the mother bird—a black bird with red wings—returned to the nest and the baby bird explained what had happened. "I was so excited to fly that I jumped out of the nest and I couldn't get back. That nice animal helped me."

"Well, I thank you very, very much," the mother bird said to

Hodgepodge. "I'm afraid my son is a little too eager to fly."

"You might not believe this, but I do know how that feels," said Hodgepodge.

"My name is Shadow," said the mother bird.

"And I am Hodgepodge."

Shadow looked at Hodgepodge for a long moment. "You look very familiar. I remember a hippo who looked a lot like you—a female. A mother hippo, in fact. This was some time ago."

"Here? In the jungle?"

"Yes, yes. And the resemblance is amazing. I'm just wondering—"

"I was born in the jungle," Hodgepodge said.

"Oh my," said Shadow. "So it is you!"

Hodgepodge was stunned. "What do you mean?"

Shadow hesitated and finally said: "You were born right here—just about where you are standing. I saw it happen."

"Would you tell me?"

Shadow hesitated again. "Are you sure you want to hear it?"

Hodgepodge said: "Yes. I must hear it. Please."

"I was here in my nest when I first saw her and I remember thinking how odd it was for a hippo to be running through the jungle, especially so late in the day. She looked very scared, as if she was running away from someone or something—but she stopped to rest under this tree. I could see that she was

exhausted; she must have been running for a long time. I also noticed that she was pregnant. And—sure enough—while she was standing there catching her breath, she cried out in pain. Then she made a bed for herself out of vines and leaves and lay down, moaning.

"Of course, being a mother myself—I felt sorry for her. So I kept an eye on her all through the night. Toward morning, she gave birth. She nursed her baby and talked to him; it was obvious that she loved him very much. And then, as the sun came up, there were noises—the sounds of hunters coming our way. Apparently they had camped nearby for the night. The hippo kissed her baby one last time, covered him up with leaves to hide him, and ran off to lead the hunters away from her child. Hodgepodge, I ... I never saw her again."

"It was her—my first mama," Hodgepodge said, quietly. "But what happened to the baby—to me?"

"I wanted to help, but I didn't know what to do," said Shadow. "So later, when you woke up and started wandering through the jungle, crying and looking for your mother, I followed you. I felt so helpless and I was afraid you would starve to death or be killed by a leopard or some other animal. I followed you for many days and, finally—one day when you were close to the savanna—I had an idea. I found a young elephant and led him to you; his mother followed. I hoped they would be a good family for you."

"Yes, they were. They took very good care of me."

"I'm glad to hear that."

Hodgepodge thanked Shadow for her help and her story, then he and Krakatoa said their good-byes.

CHAPTER FORTY-SIX
THE GREATEST MYSTERY

*"Death is a great mystery,
but it's not the greatest mystery."*
—KRAKATOA THE PARROT-POET

THAT EVENING, THEY STOPPED for the night. Krakatoa perched on a tree branch and Hodgepodge found a place to lie down. It was a cloudy night; the darkness covered them and they could see nothing—not even a star. It was very quiet.

After a while, Krakatoa heard Hodgepodge sobbing softly in the dark. "Hodgepodge, I'm sorry."

"I never even got to know her name. But at least, now, I know why she left me."

"She loved you very, very much."

"I know," said Hodgepodge. "Krakatoa, what do you think happens when someone dies?"

"Ah, that is a great mystery," said Krakatoa. "Personally, I haven't been dead yet. I have been *almost* dead—thanks to that vulture—but I think there's a big difference between dead and almost dead. So I'm not sure exactly what happens. But I do know this: There is a greater mystery than death. A much greater mystery."

"What is the much greater mystery?" Hodgepodge asked.

"Life," said Krakatoa. "Life is the greatest mystery of all. Life is the most magical stuff in the world, but no one really knows exactly what it is. You can't make life, but you can love it and cherish it. You can't keep life in a basket, but it is in you and in me and in everything around us: It's in the trees, the fireflies, the birds, all the animals—"

"Even maggots?"

"Even maggots."

Hodgepodge looked up and saw a single, bright star. "I was lucky to have such a mother, even though I never knew her."

"Yes, you were."

"And I was lucky that Mama Moxie found me and took care of me. I had two good mothers."

"Arraakk! That you did, that you did."

Hodgepodge thought some more. "The Wow Spirit was with my first mama when she was alive."

"Without a doubt," said Krakatoa.

"So ... maybe she is with the Wow Spirit now. Maybe that is why she could speak to me in my dream."

"I see no reason to disagree," said Krakatoa.

"Krakatoa—my first mama really wanted me to find the place just right, didn't she?"

"Yes," said Krakatoa. "That's why she mentioned it three times in the dream."

"So let's find it."

CHAPTER FORTY-SEVEN
DANGER AHEAD AND DANGER BEHIND

"There's a time to fight and there's a time to run."
—KRAKATOA THE PARROT-POET

EARLY THE NEXT MORNING, HODGEPODGE and Krakatoa were awakened by human voices. From the sound of it, the humans were not far away.

"Hunters!" whispered Krakatoa, hopping onto Hodgepodge's head. "Get off the path quickly—but quietly!"

Hodgepodge cut to the right and began picking his way carefully through the thick undergrowth, trying not to disturb any birds. The sight of birds taking off would definitely bring the hunters their way.

Krakatoa signaled the monkeys in the trees to be quiet. They understood. They, too, had heard the human voices.

Hodgepodge kept moving quietly, watching every step so he didn't snap a branch.

"Krakatoa," Hodgepodge whispered. "Do you think these could be the hunters that chased my first mama?"

"Could be," whispered Krakatoa. "Could be."

After a few minutes, the quiet was broken by a loud growl: "Rowwwrrr!" A leopard dropped out of a tree and landed noiselessly in front of them. Hodgepodge stopped. The leopard crouched.

"Uh-oh," said Hodgepodge. "Trouble ahead."

"And trouble behind," Krakatoa whispered. "Those hunters put a high value on leopard skins and I'm sure they heard the growl. They'll be coming this way."

The leopard growled again and crept toward them.

"I'll fight the leopard," Hodgepodge said.

"Hippos are no match for leopards," said Krakatoa. "And even if you somehow managed to beat him, the hunters will be here soon and they'll kill you. There's a time to fight and there's a time to run. This is a time to run."

But Hodgepodge didn't move.

The leopard took a step in their direction, growling low.

"Hodgepodge, what are you waiting for?" said Krakatoa. "There's an opening through the trees to the left. *Run!*"

"But the leopard will chase us and leopards are very fast," said Hodgepodge. "Faster than hippos."

Suddenly, Hodgepodge turned around and took off running—back toward the hunters.

Krakatoa squawked. "Hodgepodge! What are you doing?"

Hodgepodge said nothing; he only ran faster.

The leopard let out another growl and began to follow—slowly at first, then faster.

"The leopard is following us!" said Krakatoa.

"Good!" said Hodgepodge. He picked up speed, crashing through the bushes and trees and vines.

"Fly away!" Hodgepodge yelled to Krakatoa as he ran.

"I'm not leaving you," said Krakatoa, looking back. "But hurry! The leopard is gaining!"

"A little further now," yelled Hodgepodge, still running for all he was worth. "Hang on!"

Over a short distance, a hippo can run almost as fast as a leopard. And Hodgepodge was running as if his life depended on it—which, of course, it did.

Still, the leopard was gaining.

Moments later, the hunters—who thought they were tracking a leopard—were shocked to hear something crashing through the bushes. And then they were even more shocked to see a hippo with a parrot on his head, barreling out of the trees directly at them. They yelled out in surprise and terror and raised their spears.

In a split-second, two things happened at once: Hodgepodge swerved sharply to the left and the leopard leapt. The hunters found themselves face-to-face with a fierce, roaring, leaping leopard!

Hodgepodge crashed on through thick bushes. Behind him, the leopard roared and the hunters screamed—but no one was chasing Hodgepodge.

"Brilliant!" yelled Krakatoa.

Hodgepodge didn't stop to celebrate. He kept running until the sounds of the hunters and the leopard faded. And still he kept going, dodging in and out between trees, sniffing the air as he ran.

"I smell something," said Hodgepodge. "Just ahead."

All at once, Hodgepodge burst out of the jungle—and stopped.

There in front of him was the largest watering hole he had ever seen.

CHAPTER FORTY-EIGHT
JUMPING INTO DREAM

"Our fears are only reflections of ourselves in the waters of life. When we dare to jump into life, we become bigger than our fears."
—**KRAKATOA THE PARROT-POET**

HODGEPODGE WAS ACTUALLY LOOKING at a great, wide river—but he had never seen or heard of a river before. The most water he had ever seen was the watering hole in the savanna, which only came up to his belly.

"So ... much ... water!" said Hodgepodge, gasping for breath. "Is this a watering hole?"

"No, young Potamus. It is not."

Hodgepodge looked at Krakatoa. "You haven't called me Potamus in a while."

"Now is the right time."

"Why."

"It is part of who you are. Your mother told you that you are a hippo, but your full title is: hippopotamus."

"Hippopotamus?"

"Yes. 'Potamus' means river. What you are looking at is a river and it is your home. You must jump into it."

"What?" said Hodgepodge. He was standing on a high bank above the river. "Jump in?" He walked to the edge and looked down into the water.

"Why would I want to jump in?" he asked, studying his own reflection.

"Hippos live in this river."

Hodgepodge looked across the river. "I don't see any hippos."

"You have to jump into the river to find them. You must make your home with the hippos now."

Hodgepodge looked down. The waters looked dark and deep. He had never jumped into deep water before. "I am very heavy. I will sink to the bottom," he said. "I am too heavy to fly and too heavy to jump into a river."

"This is what you are meant to do," said Krakatoa.

Hodgepodge found this hard to believe. "I have done many crazy things, but I think jumping into a river would be the craziest thing of all."

"And, yet, this is absolutely a thing hippos do," said Krakatoa. "I would bet all my feathers on it."

"How can you be so sure?"

"Because I know the name of this river."

"What is the name?"

"Dream River."

Hodgepodge was stunned. "Dream River," he repeated. "Jump into dream ... Jump into Dream River."

"Yes," said Krakatoa. "That is what your mother was trying to tell you."

Hodgepodge stared at Krakatoa. And then, he stared at the river.

Finally, he backed up and took a deep breath. He ran across the bank, leapt, made a huge splash ... and found himself deep underwater.

Hodgepodge had never been underwater before; it felt strange and frightening. He panicked and began to frantically flail all four legs. He kicked and kicked, and then—just before he ran out of air—he found his footing and pushed upward and his head popped to the surface.

Gasping for breath, Hodgepodge paddled furiously with his legs, afraid he would sink again. When he finally realized that the water was helping to hold him up, he relaxed and began to move his legs more smoothly.

He called out, "Krakatoa! This feels amazing! I feel as light as a feather!"

He paddled some more and yelled, "Krakatoa, it feels like flying!"

But there was no answer. When Hodgepodge turned and looked back to the bank, Krakatoa was gone.

CHAPTER FORTY-NINE
SAVING SUNSHINE

*"Sometimes, to save your life,
you must be ready to lose it."*
—KRAKATOA THE PARROT-POET

"**KRAKATOA, WHERE ARE YOU?**" Hodgepodge yelled, but there was still no answer. He looked left and right. He could see the place where they came out of the jungle and the high bank where he had jumped into the river—but Krakatoa was nowhere to be seen.

Hodgepodge went back to the bank and climbed up. "Krakatoa, Krakatoa!" He walked up and down, calling for a long time. Krakatoa never answered.

The jungle was quiet. The river kept flowing.

Finally—not knowing what else to do—Hodgepodge climbed back down into the water and started up-river, looking for hippos. He wondered what he would do when he found some.

Before he had gone very far, Hodgepodge saw the first hippo he had ever seen, except for himself and his mother in the dream. It was a female hippo across the river, close to the far bank.

Excited but nervous, Hodgepodge moved across the river. As he got closer, he realized that something was wrong: The female hippo was thrashing around in a frenzy.

And then, she screamed!

Hodgepodge moved faster. When he came near, he saw what looked like a truly gigantic lizard—three or four times the size of a Komodo dragon. It had clamped its huge jaws around the hippo's hind leg and was dragging her toward the bank.

The female hippo caught sight of Hodgepodge and screamed, "Help! Help!"

Hodgepodge let out a roar and rushed to the gigantic lizard. He opened his mouth and chomped down with all his might on the lizard's neck. When the lizard opened his mouth to scream, the female hippo escaped.

The gigantic lizard lashed at Hodgepodge with his powerful tail and knocked him away, and then rushed at Hodgepodge—clamping his jaws on the hippo's front leg. Hodgepodge roared in pain and struggled to get away, but the gigantic lizard held on tight.

The fight turned into a deadly tug-of-war, with the lizard

trying to pull Hodgepodge underwater and Hodgepodge trying to pull his leg away. The harder they both pulled, the greater the pain. Hodgepodge roared and thrashed and pulled with all his might, trying to get away—but he could not get free. Slowly, slowly the gigantic lizard pulled Hodgepodge under the surface of the river.

The female hippo had moved away to a safe distance to watch. She saw the lizard and the hippo disappear. The surface of the river churned violently—evidence of the mighty struggle going on below.

Once, the giant lizard's tail broke the surface, thrashing wildly back and forth. Another time, Hodgepodge's head emerged for a moment. He gulped for air, glanced at her with frightened eyes, and was pulled under again.

The churning of the water went on and on for some time as the female hippo watched anxiously.

And then, the churning stopped. The surface was still.

The water turned red.

"Oh no!" the female hippo groaned. She saw something float to the surface. Was it the hippo?

No! It was the lifeless body of the giant lizard, belly up, floating downstream with the current.

At first, she was filled with tremendous relief—but when Hodgepodge did not appear, her relief turned to dread.

She rushed to the scene of the battle. "Where are you?

Where are you?"

Another body floated to the surface—Hodgepodge. And he, too, began to float downstream.

CHAPTER FIFTY
TEARS AND LAUGHTER

"Do you know what life is really about? It's about tears and laughter."
—KRAKATOA THE PARROT-POET

"**NOOOOO!" SCREAMED THE FEMALE HIPPO.** She rushed after Hodgepodge, but the current was so rapid that it carried both of them far downstream before she was able to catch up with him. Finally, she got ahead of Hodgepodge, then she turned around, braced her feet on the river bottom, and faced upstream. The current brought the hippo's body quickly toward her, floating sideways. She lowered her head into his side and pushed and pushed against him with all her might, trying to push the hippo's big body against the current and toward the bank. The current was strong, however, and Hodgepodge's body was heavy and slippery. As she was pushing, her head slipped and the current carried Hodgepodge past her, whirling downstream around a bend in the river.

"NOOOOO!" She screamed again. She raced downstream after Hodgepodge but, as she rounded the river bend, she saw what lay ahead. Rapids! If she didn't stop Hodgepodge now, he would soon be carried into the white water that churned and raged through rocks and boulders. He would be torn to pieces.

This was her last chance.

Running and swimming as fast as possible, she finally managed to catch up with Hodgepodge's body and then move past it. Ahead in the river, there was a large boulder that marked the beginning of the rapids. She moved quickly to the boulder, then turned around, to brace herself against it, waiting for the current to bring Hodgepodge to her.

"Oooff!" she said as Hodgepodge's heavy body floated right into her and almost knocked her off the boulder. Somehow she just managed to keep her balance. Bracing herself carefully against the slippery boulder, she lowered her head into Hodgepodge's side and pushed the hippo's body against the current with all her strength, straining with every muscle in her body. *It's impossible*, she thought. *I'm getting nowhere.* Still, she kept pushing and pushing and slowly, slowly, slowly she began to move Hodgepodge out of the rapid current toward a slower, shallower part of the river. Getting her feet onto the river bottom, she kept pushing until she succeeded in moving the body up into the very shallow water near the bank where the current couldn't take him.

And then, she collapsed, completely exhausted.

After a few minutes of rest, she struggled to her feet. Hodgepodge was lying on his back, still unconscious. "Wake up! Wake up!" she yelled. No response. "Wake up!" No response at all.

A snow-white egret was standing nearby, watching. "Roll him onto his stomach," she said.

The female hippo didn't understand this suggestion, but she had learned to trust the advice of birds. She lowered her head into Hodgepodge's side and pushed and grunted until she got him rolled over onto his stomach.

"Wake up! Wake up!" she yelled again, but Hodgepodge still did not respond. She started sobbing. "It's no use!"

"Sit on his back!" the egret said.

"What? I'll hurt him."

"No, you won't," said the egret. "He's a big guy, but he's swallowed a lot of water and you need to push it out. Sit on his back."

Desperate to try anything, she turned around and carefully sat down on Hodgepodge's back. Nothing.

"Bounce up and down a little," said the egret.

"Are you sure?"

"Yes, but hurry. There isn't much time."

She carefully bounced up and down on the hippo's back. Nothing happened.

She bounced a little harder. Hodgepodge coughed and coughed again—and then the water came gushing out of his mouth. He coughed some more and opened his eyes.

"Uh, where am I?" said Hodgepodge. He tried to move, but couldn't. "Is something on top of me?"

"Oh, excuse me," said the female hippo, getting off. "I just … well, look—you're alive!"

Hodgepodge coughed again, spit up more water, then struggled weakly to his feet. He looked around. "Where's the big lizard?"

"That was a crocodile. He's dead. He floated downstream. You almost floated with him."

"I did?"

"I pushed you up here—then I … well, the egret told me to sit on your back to, you know, push the water out. I hope I didn't hurt you."

"Oh no, I'm fine. I think." said Hodgepodge. "Uh … thank you. Thank you for pushing me up here and, um, thank you for sitting on me."

"Are you … do you think you're alright?"

Hodgepodge limped around a bit. "That crocodile chewed on my leg pretty good, but I think I'm okay. Are you all right?"

"Thanks to you!" she said. She showed him her wounded leg.

"We have matching wounds."

"I guess we saved each other," said Hodgepodge.

The female hippo grinned. "I guess we did." Then she stared at him. *"Who are you?"*

"My name is Hodgepodge. Who are you?"

"I'm Sunshine."

Hodgepodge stared at her. "Sunshine? Your name is Sunshine? Are you sure?"

Sunshine laughed. "Well, I guess I know my own name."

Hodgepodge stared some more. "Sunshine, can I ask you a question?"

"Of course."

"Where is your mother?"

Sunshine hesitated, then she said, "When I was younger, my mother disappeared. She went off into the jungle to find some food and never came back. And then, not long ago, my father died. So, I'm an orphan now, but—"

Hodgepodge interrupted her. "Your mother disappeared in the jungle?"

"Yes."

Now it was Hodgepodge's turn to hesitate. "Sunshine, was your mother expecting a child when she went into the jungle?"

"Yes, but how did you know that? Did you know my mother? Did you know Moon?"

"Your mother's name was Moon?"

"Yes."

Now, Hodgepodge understood why his mother appeared to him in the moon in his dream. He was so overcome with emotion that he couldn't speak.

"Hodgepodge, are you okay?" Sunshine asked. "Is something wrong?"

"I am her child," Hodgepodge managed to say. "I am your brother."

Sunshine was speechless. And then she started crying and laughing at the same time. The two hippos embraced and there were tears of sadness mixed with tears of joy.

After a while, Hodgepodge said, "I'll tell you the whole story soon—but, first, would you take me to meet the other hippos?"

CHAPTER FIFTY-ONE
THE PLACE JUST RIGHT

"The journey to the place just right is not just about finding a place.
It's about becoming the 'me' you always wished you could be."
—**KRAKATOA THE PARROT-POET**

AS THE TWO LIMPING, EXHAUSTED hippos moved upriver, Sunshine talked excitedly and Hodgepodge took it all in—the peaceful river flowing around them, the sunbeams dancing on the water, the happy cries of birds circling and diving for fish, and the sound of Sunshine's voice.

My sister, he thought. *My very own sister. My very own family.*

"The tribe is pretty cool," she said. "Well, most of them anyway. Later I'll tell you which ones to watch out for."

They came around a bend and what did they see in the river ahead? A whole tribe of hippos!

Hodgepodge stopped. He was overwhelmed. "I've never

seen any other hippos before today," he told Sunshine. "I want to meet them, but I'm nervous. I don't know if I will fit in. I'm not very good at fitting in."

"No worries," said Sunshine. "You'll fit in just fine. They'll be excited to meet you."

"They will?"

"Are you kidding? Of course, they will."

"Sunshine, I've waited my whole life for this."

"Hey, they're just hippos. Let's go."

As they approached, Glory, the oldest hippo, called out: "Sunshine, you had me worried sick! You know you're not supposed to go off by yourself."

"Aunt Glory, everyone—I want you to meet Hodgepodge," said Sunshine, eager to change the subject.

"Funny name for a hippo," said Aunt Glory, looking him over with a critical eye. "Where did you come from, Hodgepodge?" She did not sound pleased to meet him.

Hodgepodge looked nervously around and said, "Actually, it's a long story—"

Sunshine interrupted. "He's my brother! Moon gave birth to him in the jungle."

Glory turned to Hodgepodge. "Is this true? Are you Moon's child?"

"Yes," said Hodgepodge. "When Mama gave birth to me ... well, there were hunters nearby. She ran off to lead the hunters away and she never came back. I was found and raised by elephants."

Glory stared at Hodgepodge for a long moment. Then she broke into a big hippo smile. "Well, as a matter of fact, you look just like Moon, don't you? Welcome home, Hodgepodge! You'll have to tell us your story."

That evening, all the hippos climbed out onto the riverbank and Hodgepodge told the whole story from the time Moxie found him in the jungle to the time when he jumped into the river. The hippos were amazed—they had never heard of a hippo who had traveled so far and had so many adventures.

"Actually, that's not quite the whole story," said Sunshine. "Hodgepodge saved my life." She proceeded to tell how Hodgepodge saved her from the crocodile and how she had saved him from drowning.

After Sunshine's story, Glory spoke up. "Hodgepodge, you have come along at just the right time. Those crocodiles have been getting meaner and bolder and we could use some help fighting them off."

"I would be honored to help," said Hodgepodge. All of the hippos cheered and, if you ever have an opportunity to hear hippos cheering, it is a sound you will never forget.

Over the next few days, Hodgepodge got to know all of the hippos in the tribe and he learned how to do the things hippos do. Sunshine told him stories about his mother and father—stories that helped fill some empty places in his heart.

Every morning and evening, Hodgepodge would travel up and down the river, looking for crocodiles and practicing his roar. The crocs soon learned that the hippos had a brave new defender and they once again kept their distance.

So the hippo tribe of Dream River lived in peace, and Hodgepodge no longer felt like the only hippo in the world. At last, he was in the place just right.

Time passed as it always does, and Hodgepodge was so busy and so happy with his new life that he rarely thought about his old days on the savanna or his time going through the jungle with Krakatoa.

Until …

CHAPTER FIFTY-TWO
THE BOY IN THE VILLAGE

"The fun is in the finding and the joy is in the journey."
—KRAKATOA THE PARROT-POET

ONE EVENING—MANY MOONS later—when Hodgepodge was relaxing in the middle of the river, he looked up and saw two elephants on the bank. A parrot was sitting on top of one of the elephants. Hodgepodge moved quickly toward them.

"It *is* you!" he said, climbing up onto the bank to greet Mama Moxie and Bump and Krakatoa.

"I thought you might want to see your adopted family again—so I brought them," Krakatoa explained.

"On the way here, Krakatoa told us all about your journey," said Mama Moxie. Then she fixed a stern eye on Hodgepodge,

"You broke the rule about going into the jungle! You worried me to death!"

Hodgepodge said, "Yes, Mama Moxie, I'm sorry. I was—"

"A little crazy!" said Bump.

"Yes, that's it," said Hodgepodge.

"Well, once in a while, the wrong thing turns out to be the right thing," Moxie said. "I guess this is one of those times."

"Mama, you forgot to tell him that we broke the rule, too—so we could come here," Bump said. "The jungle was amazing!"

Moxie said, "Yes, it was. A little scary at times, but amazing."

"How are things on the savannah?" Hodgepodge asked. "How are Humdrum and Muzzle and VanDerMugg and Sniff and Scab?"

"Ornery as ever!" said Moxie. "I think they did feel a little bad about the way they treated you—especially after the terrible scolding I gave them for running you off."

"So if I came back—?"

"Oh, they would accept you now. But, you know old Scab—he'll never admit he was wrong. I think it would break his face if he did."

"I might come for a visit someday, if Krakatoa would guide me," said Hodgepodge. He added, "Mama Moxie, I never said thank you for saving me from the jungle and raising me. So thank you. Thank you very much."

Moxie smiled and gave him a loving tap with her trunk. "It was a joy," she said. "An interesting joy, but a joy."

"What's life like in the river?" said Bump. "What do you do all the time?"

"Mostly, I watch out for crocodiles," said Hodgepodge. "Sometimes I fight them."

"What's a crocodile?"

"It's sort of like the most gigantic lizard you could imagine," Hodgepodge said.

"So you finally got over your fear of lizards?"

"Yes, Just Bump."

"I told you—my name is just Bump," said Bump, grinning.

Hodgepodge grinned. "That is what I said."

Over the next few days, Hodgepodge introduced Moxie and Bump to the hippos in his tribe and they all had a great time. The elephants even joined the hippos in the river for some hippo games.

Finally, Moxie and Bump said their good-byes and left to make the journey back to the savanna, but Krakatoa stayed behind.

That night, sitting on the riverbank, Hodgepodge said, "Krakatoa, you helped me stay on the journey even when I was being hard-headed."

"Sometimes, a hard head comes in handy," said Krakatoa. "Like when you head-butted the Komodo dragon."

"I guess that's true. But I do have one question."

"I'd be all ears—if I had ears."

"You knew all along that we were headed to Dream River, didn't you?"

"I confess—I did," said Krakatoa.

"Why didn't you tell me where we were going?"

"The fun is in the finding and the joy is in the journey. It was more exciting for you to discover it at the end, don't you think?"

Hodgepodge nodded. "I guess it was."

"Plus—if I had tried to explain about the river, you wouldn't have understood. You found it hard to understand even when you were looking right at it."

"True."

"But the main reason was this: You needed time to learn to listen to your Wow and prepare yourself for the challenges ahead."

Hodgepodge's small ears twitched. "How can I ever repay you?"

Krakatoa looked out at the river. "Just pass along to the young hippos some of the things you've learned. Teach them to listen to their Wow."

"That I will gladly do."

The two friends spent a long time rehashing many memories from their journey together. Finally Hodgepodge said:

"It is a funny thing. The journey through the jungle was the most difficult, frightening thing I've ever done. But it was also *splendiferous*!"

"Arraakk! It was! It was!" said Krakatoa, bobbing his head.

They sat in silence for a while, watching the river go by. Finally, Krakatoa said, "I must be going. There is a boy in a village who needs to hear your story."

Krakatoa turned to face the hippo. "Hodgepodge, your mother would be proud of you. She would see the spark in your eye." And then, Krakatoa the parrot-poet flew away into the darkness.

Late into the night, Hodgepodge sat alone on the high bank watching the full moon rise over Dream River. The moonlight danced on the surface of the water. A fish jumped for joy. The flowing river whispered, hinting at secrets it had kept for thousands of years.

And then, a familiar face appeared in the moon.

"Mama?" Hodgepodge called.

The face said nothing. It only smiled, then winked ... and then faded.

Hodgepodge whispered, "Wow."

Epilogue

• • •

IT IS LATE AT NIGHT in the village of Bahati when Hekima finishes. The fire burns low. The people are quiet, thinking about the story. A baby cries softly. A songbird calls to its mate. A shooting star flashes across the sky.

After a few moments, Hekima says, "And that, my friends, is the end of Hodgepodge's story and the beginning of the story of our new year together. And here is my wish for each one of you: This year, may there be a spark in your eye, a song in your heart, and a spring in your step. And, no matter what may happen—no matter how many troubles we may face—may we always listen to the Wow that is in us."

The people rise and walk through the darkened streets to their huts, singing softly the song of the Wow. The sound of their voices mingles with the smoke from the fire and rises into the night sky under a million stars.

THE END

HE IS SPUNKY.
HE IS ADVENTURESOME.
HE WANTS TO SAVE THE WORLD.
THERE'S JUST ONE PROBLEM.
HE'S A MOSQUITO.

Izzy Mosquito has a problem. He dreams of going on great adventures and righting the wrongs of the world—but everyone thinks he's just a pest! To make matters worse, a war breaks out between the animals and the mosquitoes at Pickle Pond Farm and Izzy is declared a traitor by the High Mosquito Council!

Meanwhile, Izzy's beloved but addled grandmother, Gitche Manito Mosquito, tells Izzy that it's up to him to stop the war and save the farm. But Izzy has no idea how to do that.

Turn the page for an excerpt...

COMING IN THE FALL OF 2020

IZZY'S IMPOSSIBLE ADVENTURE

GEOFFERY ALAN MOORE

"WHAT THE STINKING MAGGOT WAS I THINKING?"

IZZY MOSQUITO BUZZED ACROSS *the countryside following the trail of scorched and smoking villages. He was tempted to stop at each burnt town and check for survivors, but he didn't—for two reasons.*

First, if he found any humans, they might swat him.

Second, there was no time. He had to find the fire-breathing dragon FAST.

"How on earth did I get myself into this?" Izzy thought as he flew.

But of course, he knew how.

Only the day before, King Alfred had asked for volunteers to fight the giant dragon that was terrorizing the kingdom. All of his knights had tried to stop the monster and, one by one, they had been scorched, torched, roasted, toasted, fried, or burnt to a cinder.

The dragon had turned them all into charred knight-kebabs. There were no knights left. Zero. Zilch. None.

So the King was desperate. Very desperate.

"I'm begging you," the King said in a speech to his subjects. "Please, please, please, pretty please, someone stop this horrible dragon before it incinerates our entire kingdom. If you volunteer, I will make you a knight immediately and I will even put 'sir' in front of your name. So who will volunteer? Anyone? Anyone want to be a knight? I'll take absolutely anyone—old, lame, on crutches, whatever. Anyone at all?"

Dead silence. No volunteers.

Then Izzy buzzed up to the throne. He dodged an attempted swat by the King's chief adviser and landed on top of the king's scepter. "I'll go," he said.

"Did I hear something?" said the King, looking around.

Izzy yelled, "I'LL GO!"

"You?" said the King, looking down his nose at Izzy. "You're a speck, a bug, a pest!" All the king's advisors laughed.

"Please, your honor," Izzy said. "I've always dreamed of becoming a knight. This is my only chance! And besides, what have you got to lose?"

Izzy had a point. It was a crazy point, but it was a point.

"Oh, all right," the king said. "By royal decree I dub thee an official knight, which title you may wear for the rest of your short life, blah, blah, blah. Now, go destroy that dragon!"

"I won't let you down, oh, King," Izzy said.

"Well, we'll see about that," the King whispered to his chief advisor.

As Izzy set out on his journey, the advisors chuckled but the people cheered.

But now, as he flew across the countryside alone, there were no cheers or chuckles—only cries and moans and barking dogs and smoke rising from one burnt village after another.

Then, through the thick morning fog mixed with smoke, Izzy saw a sight that turned his thorax cold: A streak of fire slashed across the sky and crashed into another village, setting it ablaze.

Izzy hurried in the direction of the fire. There was no time to lose.

Suddenly, an ungodly dragon scream came out of the haze. It sounded as if the earth had split open to release a belching roar from hell.

Actually, it sounded something like this: AAAAAUUURRRRG-GGHHHEEEEEYIIIIIEEEEE!

Anyway, it didn't sound good.

Next there was an earth-shaking BOOM! BOOM! BOOM! BOOM! BOOM!

The dragon was climbing up the slope toward the glorious city of Eternia which was built on top of the highest mountain in the kingdom.

"At least it's a non-flying dragon," Izzy said. "I guess that's something to be thankful for." Izzy was trying to look on the bright side.

The fog-mixed-with-smoke was so thick that Izzy could hardly see anything, so he buzzed up the side of the mountain following the hideous sound of the dragon's screams. But when he came to the top and neared the gates of the great city, Izzy got his first glimpse of the gigantic monster.

It was far more terrifying than anything he had ever imagined. It was black and slimy and huge—as tall as the walls around the city.

Izzy had only one thought: "What the stinking maggot was I thinking?"

GRUMPY GAS BAG

...

THE BEAST LET OUT ANOTHER *bone-chilling scream and unleashed a sulfurous blast of fire against the city gates. Fortunately, the iron gates held.*

The dragon screamed again and started battering the gates with his huge, powerful tail: BAM! BAM! BAM! BAM! BAM! BAM! BAM! BAM! BAM!

The gates creaked, the wall shook, stones began to crumble and fall.

Inside, even the bravest men of the city were crying and running in every direction, looking for places to hide.

But there is no hiding from a giant, fire-breathing dragon.

Everyone in the city heard the dragon screaming and battering the gate. They could feel the ground shake. They knew it was only a matter of time. Maybe only a matter of minutes.

Izzy watched the dragon, feeling helpless. What could he do?

And then, he noticed something. Every time the dragon slammed his tail against the wall and it did not collapse, he screamed in anger and irritation.

"He gets irritated easily," Izzy thought. "And when he gets irritated, he gets really upset. He's a big baby!"

This gave Izzy an idea. He flew straight at the dragon's head and began buzzing circles around his eyes and ears.

Now, everyone knows that the sound of a mosquito buzzing is the most irritating sound on planet earth. No creature can stand it—not even a dragon. So as soon as Izzy started buzzing, the evil dragon stopped banging on the gate. He started whirling around and around, snapping at Izzy. But Izzy was too quick for him—and he was careful to stay away from the dragon's fiery mouth.

This drove the dragon absolutely berserk. He kept whirling around and around and around, faster and faster as Izzy circled his head again and again.

When Izzy saw that the dragon was very furious, very irritated, and very dizzy, he flew over the edge of the cliff, just beyond the city wall, and taunted the dragon, "Come and get me you grumpy gas bag!"

Standing at the edge of the cliff, the dragon unleashed a furious volley of fire but he was so dizzy that his aim was off. He missed Izzy completely.

Izzy flew a little farther out and taunted him again. "What's the matter? Afraid to fight a tiny mosquito? You're no dragon; you're just a big drag!"

By this time, the world was spinning wildly for the dragon. He shook his head, tried to clear his eyes and focus. He saw the mosquito, dancing in mid-air, just out of reach, making fun of him.

Beside himself with anger and frustration, the dragon lunged at the mosquito ... and fell over the side of the cliff!

Down, down, down the beast fell, screaming all the way until he crashed far below, in a puff of smoke. The screaming stopped.

Soldiers who had been watching from the top of the city walls saw what happened and reported it to the people. The city leaders opened the gates and crowds cheered and welcomed Izzy as a hero, chanting, "Izzy! Izzy! Izzy!"

"YOU'LL FIND OUT ON THE FOURTH OF JULY"

• • •

"**IZZY, IZZY, IZZY, WAKE UP!**"

Izzy Mosquito opened his eyes; it was his mother.

"Get up, dear. It's time to go pester some animals."

It's that crazy dream again, Izzy thought. He'd had the dream about the dragon before, but he'd told no one except his beloved grandmother, Gitche Manito Mosquito.

Gitche was the oldest mosquito in the tribe—almost three months old! She was famous because she had been swatted nine times and survived—three times by humans, twice by a cow, once by a donkey, twice by a dog, and once by a llama.

Unfortunately, these swats left Gitche a little addled and very hard of hearing. Still, Izzy loved talking with her.

"Gitche, can you help me understand my dream," Izzy asked her one time.

"What's that? Cream? There is not much to understand about cream, Izzy. It's not as tasty as cow's blood or daisy nectar, but it'll do."

Izzy raised his voice. "Excuse me, Gitche, I mean DREAM! I keep having a DREAM about a DRAGON!" Izzy explained the dream to Gitche, as loud as he could. "What do you think it means, Gitche?"

Gitche sighed and smiled. "I think it means you are going to do something very special someday. But I could be wrong. I'm just an old grandmother."

"But ... but what am I going to do?"

Gitche tilted her head back, closed her eyes, smiled, and said the words that would change Izzy's life: *"You'll find out on the fourth of July."*

GEOFFERY ALAN MOORE worked as a copywriter and creative director for ad agencies in New York City. He is the author of *The Tale of Hodgepodge* and *Izzy Saves The Galaxy*. Geoffery and his wife, Sharon, now make their home in Baltimore.

For a discussion guide to *The Tale Of Hodgepodge*, plus information on upcoming books, see: www.GeofferyMoore.com

For more information about Living Conversation Books and The Living Conversation blog, see: TheLivingConversation.com